One Of Three

by

George O. Smith

One Of Three
by George O. Smith

Copyright © 2024

All Rights reserved.

No part of this publication may be reproduced, stored in a retrieval system, or transmitted in any form or by any means, electronic, mechanical, photocopying or Otherwise, without the written permission of the publisher.
The author/editor asserts the moral right to be identified as the author/editor of this work.

ISBN: 978-93-64282-63-5

Published by

DOUBLE 9 BOOKS

2/13-B, Ansari Road
Daryaganj, New Delhi – 110002
info@double9books.com
www.double9books.com
Tel. 011-40042856

This book is under public domain

ABOUT THE AUTHOR

George Oliver Smith was an American science fiction author. He was born on April 9, 1911, and died on May 27, 1981. He was also known by the pen name Wesley Long. He is not to be confused with American science fiction writer George H. Smith. During the Golden Age of Science Fiction in the 1940s, Smith wrote for the magazine Astounding Science Fiction. John W. Campbell, Jr., the editor of the magazine, stopped working with him when Campbell's first wife, Doa, left him and married Smith in 1949. Smith kept putting out science fiction books and stories on a regular basis until 1960. During the 1960s and 1970s, when he had a job that needed his full attention, he didn't get as much done. In 1980, he got the first award from the Fandom Hall of Fame. He was a member of the Trap Door Spiders, an all-male literary club. Isaac Asimov's Black Widowers, a fictional group of people who solve crimes, were based on the Trap Door Spiders. Smith mostly wrote about space, like in Operation Interstellar (1950), Lost in Space (1959), and Troubled Star (1957).

ABOUT THE AUTHOR

George Oliver Smith was an American science fiction author. He was born on April 9, 1911, and died on May 27, 1981. He was also known by the pen name Wesley Long. He is not to be confused with American science fiction writer George H. Smith. During the Golden Age of Science Fiction in the 1940s, Smith wrote for the magazine Astounding Science Fiction. John W. Campbell, Jr., the editor of the magazine, stopped working with him when Campbell's first wife, Doa, left him and married Smith in 1949. Smith kept putting out science fiction books and stories on a regular basis until 1960. During the 1960s and 1970s, when he had a job that needed his full attention, he didn't get as much done. In 1980, he got the first award from the Fandom Hall of Fame. He was a member of the Trap Door Spiders, an all-male literary club. Isaac Asimov's Black Widowers, a fictional group of people who solve crimes, were based on the Trap Door Spiders. Smith mostly wrote about space, like in Operation Interstellar (1950), Lost in Space (1959), and Troubled Star (1957).

CONTENTS

Chapter I
Contact!

The bit of whitish substance fluoresced, which of course was quite natural. It also vibrated very faintly, which was unnatural. At least, this property had not been known previously—which is really saying little since the material had been compounded from artificial radioisotopes from the big piles. All too little was known about such items and the fact that this one was vibrating ever so faintly whenever the electron beam struck it was interesting both from a scientific and a lay curiosity standpoint.

Ed Bronson blinked a bit and decided that he had made some mistake. It had ceased to vibrate.

Ed cracked the experimental tube and removed the irregular lump. It had been hoped to produce a more brilliant and higher-contrast phosphor for television screens. But if it was going to vibrate—

Ed inserted the lump of phosphor back in the tube, pumped it and restarted the whole gear.

It vibrated again, ever so faintly, against the bottom of the glass. Bronson listened carefully, his engineer's mind trying to identify the sound. It was not the sixteen kilocycle sweep circuit—not the one that scanned the face of the television tube, because this was not a complete set-up and there was no scanning energy necessary. It was vaguely familiar.

It came and it went, that faint vibration. Sometimes it rattled violently, other times it purred gently. Always very faintly of course—for the term 'violently' means only by comparison.

Ed adjusted the field strength of the focusing magnet about the neck of the tube and the vibration strengthened to a noticeable degree. He juggled the controls but found he had hit the maximum or optimum response.

There was something about it.... It was like human whisperings too faint to be understood but not too faint to be unheard. Like the bloop-bleep of a leaky faucet that seems to be saying things about you just too quietly to be really understood. Like the imagined whisperings heard by the paranoiac....

Ed laughed. Hearing things!

Like hades he was hearing things. It was really there. The lump of phosphor moved a perceptible amount as a peak of rattle passed. And yet....

Ed Bronson uncoiled his wiry six feet from the chair and cracked the seal on the tube again. He lifted the top and squinted at the crystalline whiteness that had been rattling so maddeningly.

He went to a cupboard at the end of his laboratory and rummaged among small boxes that stood on one shelf—no two boxes seeming to be of the same size. The upshot of this rummaging was that Bronson had to spend some time repiling the boxes after he had found the contact microphone he was seeking. Eventually, however, Ed Bronson was repumping the tube.

Inside was the crystal phosphor and fastened to it was a sensitive contact microphone.

Once more Bronson keyed the switches, adjusted focus, and intensity. Then, from the speaker of the amplifier connected to the contact microphone, there came a cacophony of noise, howling whistles, deep-throated hums, and a horde of middle-register tones. Not music, and far from it. Just random—somethings.

Yet in the background, barely audible as such but most definitely identifiable, was the voice of a woman.

Any speaker would have ceased had she known her efforts were thus wasted. It was indistinguishable and unintelligible save for a scattered word here and there, which was unmistakably in English. Ed Bronson thought that it was like trying to eavesdrop on a conversation in a boiler factory.

He wondered what radio program he had tapped in on. He turned his radio on, and scanned the bands, even listening to the weaker stations— which, of course were far from being as ragged as this, regardless of their weakness—but came to the conclusion that there was nothing on the air that corresponded to the voice of the woman that emerged from his kinescope testing tube.

Bronson noted with questing interest that occasionally one or more of the interfering hoots, sirens and honks would cease for a moment or two. So also did the woman's voice. Ed prayed that when sufficient interference would cease, the woman would not choose that moment to cease also. He wanted to know more about this. There was more to it than met the eye.

If he could identify the speaker he might be able to establish a means of communication. Location was also important. Furthermore, if this were telephone or radio, he had a new means of receiving both. If it were telephone and it worked on any or all, Ed Bronson had a gadget that would make him the bane of all lovers of secrecy—including espionage agents, who, of course, hate penetration of their own little conclaves as deeply as they try to penetrate others'.

He—well, if it were radio he was intercepting he had nothing as interesting as a telephone tapping gadget. But....

The tones dropped in volume. A shrill whistle that made vicious interference with his hearing suddenly keyed off like the turning off of a light. A booming roar ceased also and others of less importance dropped or died. The cumulative effect of this was to permit the woman's voice to come through.

It was not the perfect voice of a magnificent contralto reproduced on the finest radio gear but a cool, clear contralto, transmitted by cheap, shoddy equipment and received on something both obsolete and inefficient.

Yet is was a woman's voice. And, with the luck of the patient scientist, she was saying, "... home? It's at Thirteen forty-seven Vermont Street, Postal Zone Eleven...."

And that was the first complete reception Ed Bronson heard. For, with the completion of the message, the cacophony of hoots, keenings and sirens blasted forth like a mad, insane symphony.

"I live at Thirteen forty-eight Vermont," shouted Bronson. "Across the street!"

He charged out, raced across the street and pressed the doorbell. He waited a moment and an elderly man came to the door.

"I'm Ed Bronson," explained he.

"I know you," snapped the other man. "Always gumming up my radio with your fool experiments. What do you want?"

"Is your daughter using the telephone?" he asked.

"She ain't home."

"Your wife?"

"She's with Regina."

"Well, was some woman using the—"

"Look, Bronson, I ain't got no women here when my wife ain't, see? Now what's your idea, huh?"

Bronson looked apologetic. This was Mr. Lewis McManner and both he and his family were the kind of people—one of which seems to live on every block—who chase robins from the front yard, call the police for ball-playing boys and manage to maintain an immaculate house because it never has a good chance to get cluttered with people.

"I've been working on an idea," he told McManner, "and I seem to have picked up someone who claimed that her address was Thirteen forty-seven Vermont Street."

"You'd think this was the only Vermont Street in the world!" snorted McManner, slamming the door.

Bronson turned from the front door and retraced his steps. Despite his disappointment, he could not help but grin at himself. After all, how many 1347 Vermont Streets might there be between Puget Sound and Key West? And, were he to try mailing each a letter, someone would most certainly object loudly enough to cause Ed Bronson to explain that he had heard a woman's voice mention the number and that he wanted to meet her. He could visualize the psychiatric ward looming to receive him while they tapped his knees and inspected his brain to find out whether he was safe to let loose without a muzzle.

Yet Bronson sobered soon enough. He was an engineer. He knew that what had been done once could be done again. Perhaps the way to get in touch with this woman was to try to tap back. At least he could listen to everything she said in the hope that she would repeat other information.

With a prayer Bronson separated a sizable hunk of the phosphor to work upon, while the other "sang." He breathed no sigh of relief until he had half of the original phosphor back in the tube with the works completely covered, as before, by the mad mass of meaningless hoots and catcalls. Then he went to work on the other piece. He did have a parallel set-up right on the same bench. There was something about this....

During the hours that followed there were three breaks in the whistlings. The first produced only the words "nature of the situation—" The second time the woman said, "—something *must* be done, of course, but you tell me what. I—" which also left Bronson completely in the dark. The third time, she said "—so this part of the Carlson family is going to bed!"

After which there was no woman's voice riding along with the myriad of sounds. They were as before, like a radio that has gone off the air, leaving an increased racket of background noise. It was maddening and futile.

All he had to show for her hours of telephoning was her name. Carlson.

All he had to do was to get the telephone directories of all the cities in the United States of America and perhaps Canada, then run through the listings of 'Carlson' until he hit one that lived on 1347 Vermont Street.

It might as well have been 'Smith' as far as running them down went. He could try Central City. After all, he could easily have made an error in listening.

But that was futile. Bronson sought the entire list of Carlsons and found none who lived on Vermont Street or any phonetic variation. Grumbling and baffled, he returned to his labors.

That, at least, proved more profitable. It was midnight when Bronson discovered that tapping one of the bits of phosphor caused a response in the other when they were energized by the electron bombardment from the television tube works.

From that point to vibrating the hunk of phosphor with the adapted insides of an old earphone and getting a response, took another hour of whittling, filing and working. He discarded that method of modulation two hours later when he discovered that an audio modulation of the electron stream in the kinescope tube produced the same effect.

Then, dead tired, Ed Bronson went to bed. He'd have called the woman right then and there had she been handy, but she had gone.

Bronson was truly beat. Had he stopped to think about it he would have known that something big was in the wind. For he was tapping no telephones. He had accidentally discovered some sort of communication receiving principle and had then devised a transmitter.

His first thought on the following morning was to try the receiver. She was there, all right, and so was a hooting cry of the dissonant pipe-organings.

Bronson shrugged and fired up his transmitting gadget. "Miss Carlson!" he called into the microphone. "Calling Miss Carlson of Thirteen forty-seven Vermont Street. Can you hear me?"

Then he listened.

Her voice paused briefly, took a new tone, but was still covered by the whinings.

"Miss Carlson, this is Ed Bronson. I cannot hear you clearly because of much interference. If you can hear me, make a lilting rill with your voice. This I can distinguish among the many stable-toned notes that are coming in at the time."

The voice rilled up and down several times. Then there was considerable speech which Bronson could not understand.

The upshot of this, however, was a gradual shutting down of the hootings and honkings until the receiver was clear. Then her voice came through again.

"Mr. Bronson. I have requested silence for one minute. Where are you?"

"Thirteen forty-eight Vermont Street, Central City Eleven."

"That is across the street," she said.

"Perhaps," he answered.

"Well, it is," she said. "Unless we're in different Central Cities."

"Central City, New Mexico, eighteen miles from Albuquerque?"

"That's it. But we have little time, really, because we didn't get the clear as soon as we asked for it. They hung over a bit—the commercials, I mean."

"Commercials?" he asked. Dumfounded, he began to wonder. Commercial, in radio parlance, meant any transmitter on the air for commercial purpose and the presupposition that this system of communications must be quite well known.

How then had Ed Bronson, an electronics engineer, managed to live through the commercialization of an entirely new field of communications?

"The commercial laboratories," she said.

"Oh? Then this is a laboratory experiment?"

"More than that—"

Bronson heard with dismay the first thin whistle resume.

He interrupted.

"Miss Carlson," he pleaded quickly, "we're going to be cut off again. Meet me on the corner of Vermont and Thirteenth, please?"

"Yes but—"

That was all. The keening, piping howl came with ear-shattering loudness once more.

Bronson turned off his gear and headed for the corner of Vermont and 13th. Let 'em hoot and howl.

He'd speak to the girl in person!

An hour later, Ed Bronson still stood there, leaning disconsolately against a lamp post in the bright daylight. A ring of cigarette butts surrounded his feet.

Whatever it was it was important and he, Bronson, had the key. All he had to do was to find the door!

Bronson returned home. The trouble—one of them, anyway—was that his amplifier was a high fidelity affair, capable of flat transmission of sounds as far as the human ear could hear.

That made for good music and that's what the amplifier had been built for.

So Bronson went home determined to build a series of sharp filters. First he would curtail the band-width of the amplifier until it peaked around eight hundred cycles per second, near the musical note 'A' one octave above the standard Concert Pitch 'A'.

Then he would build a set of sharply-tuned filters that would cut 'holes' in the remaining spectrum where the tonal interferences came. It would make her speech less natural but far more intelligible.

Bronson needed more evidence before he did anything serious about it.

It was nearing five o'clock in the morning before he finished his job, and started to listen once more.

Chapter II
The Red Sky

The girl turned from the window, where the bright sky silhouetted her slender figure.

"How do I know where he is?" she snapped.

"Now look, Virginia," objected one of the men in the room, "there's no point in getting angry. We must know."

"I know you must, Peter," she returned. "I agree. But I don't know. Do you understand that? I don't know!"

Peter Moray shrugged. "Anybody capable of building a space resonator must have enough training to have known about it in the first place."

John Cauldron spoke sharply, "You went out to the corner as suggested?"

"I did. He did not appear. After I returned I watched at regular intervals. No one came. Also I listened carefully as you suggested. He hasn't been calling—hasn't called since about eleven o'clock this morning."

Peter Moray smiled. "Yesterday morning," he corrected.

"Don't be funny. You're the ones that have kept me up all night asking fool questions over and over."

"They're not fool questions, Virginia."

"Any question repeated too often becomes a fool question," she replied.

Cauldron spoke heavily. "We're not cross-examining you, Virginia. Please believe that. We ask and ask and ask because it may be that something might have been said that sounds trivial, but may make large sense."

The girl shrugged. "You're entitled to try," she said. She passed a hand across her face wearily. "You've heard and reheard our conversation as verbatim as I recall it. And it was an experience I will not forget easily."

"Agreed," said Moray, walking to the west window and looking out. "I guess we're all overkeyed."

Cauldron grumbled a bit. "There have been a lot of strange things happening," he said. "This isn't the first."

Virginia smiled wanly but it was Cauldron who spoke next after a short pause. "And at five-thirty in the morning, everything begins to get somewhat distorted from a mental standpoint."

Moray turned from the brightness of the sky and mumbled something about life's lowest ebb occurring just before dawn.

Then he added, "Why did this mess have to happen? Blast it, everybody that knew swore up and down that the possibility was nil."

"Not nil enough," said Cauldron.

"No," agreed Virginia. "But that's life."

Moray slammed his fist down on the window-sill and swore. "That's life," he echoed in a mocking tone. "Well, I don't like it!"

"Who does?" demanded Cauldron quietly.

"Can't you face facts?" snapped Moray. "Do you realize that we haven't much time left? And what are we doing about it? Where are we? Nowhere, or no further along than we were thirty years ago—exactly thirty years ago. It's July sixteenth right now, and that's—"

"You're talking like a fool, Moray," said Virginia. "Have you ever stopped to think that those of us who do not rant and rave and worry ourselves into ulcers may have faced the fact, and find it ungood? Well, there are those of us who will do what we can. There's little sense in worrying about conditions—all it does is remove you from your highest efficiency.

"When something is awry you do something to correct it if you can. If you cannot you pigeonhole it until such a time as you can solve it. Not forget it, never for a moment. But there's no sense in dragging a worry back and forth across the floor until it is draining your life's blood. As for that out there, I didn't do it."

"Good for you, Virginia," applauded Cauldron.

"No," snapped Moray. "You didn't. You were not born at that time. But you can't fold your hands and accept it—nor can you say that it is none of your business!"

"There's always suicide," said Virginia Carlson.

A clock in the lower part of the house chimed once, marking the hour of five-thirty.

Moray returned to the window and looked at the sky, west. "At five-thirty in the morning of July sixteenth," he said, "one hundred and twenty miles southeast of Albuquerque, in a remote section of the Alamogordo air base, a group of scientists released the first atomic fire. Thirty years later," he finished bitterly, "we have a perpetual sunrise!"

On the laboratory table, the receiver rattled loudly. They turned, as one.

"Look," snapped Cauldron quickly, "if that is this Ed Bronson character, get in touch with him. We can use any technician we can get our hands on. Any man with a brain might well hold the key to that living cancer out there that is burning up the very earth."

"I'll put my chances on a space rocket," replied Peter Moray.

"I'd rather stop that fire out there."

"Why?" demanded Moray.

"Where would you go?" snapped Cauldron angrily. "There isn't a planet fit for human occupation and you know it. You'll either put it out or we'll all die. Not a chance for escape in any other way."

"I—"

"Shut up, while Virginia answers Bronson. He's having interference trouble—you'll make it no easier."

From the speaker was coming Ed Bronson's voice, calling for Miss Carlson and requesting an answer, for he had filters installed that eliminated the whistlings.

Cauldron jabbed Moray with an elbow. "He's a right bright fellow," he observed in a whisper.

Virginia Carlson spoke into the microphone. "You're right on the big moment," she told Bronson.

"Big moment?" he replied.

"Sure. Thirty years ago today—this moment."

"Yeah?" drawled Bronson. "And what happened?"

Peter Moray looked at John Cauldron. "Tell me," he snapped, "what kind of man could live to maturity and not know Alamogordo?"

"I don't know. I can't imagine," replied John Cauldron. "But maybe—just maybe—it is the answer we've been seeking."

Ed Bronson shook his head though he knew that the girl could not see him. He had not heard Moray or Cauldron mention Alamogordo. He repeated his query.

"And what happened?"

Virginia Carlson told him, "Thirty years ago, at Alamogordo, the scientists first released the energy from the atom."

"Oh," he replied. "I didn't know it was marked on the calendar as a holiday."

"Holiday?" exploded Virginia.

"Well?"

"That atomic fire is still burning!" snapped Virginia.

"Oh, no!"

"Well, I'm within a hundred and thirty miles of it," she replied, "and I can see it out of the window."

"Where the dickens are you?" he asked.

"You know my address," she replied.

"Yes," he agreed. "And I went there and got pushed in the face for my trouble."

"And the people who live at your address are named Carrington, not Bronson."

"How old are you?" asked Bronson.

"Twenty-five—why?"

"Look," he said, "if that atomic fire is running out there, then how did the World War Two end?"

"They brought high officials over to see the awful pillar of fire. They didn't tell them that the atomic flame would eventually eat the earth—so surrender was a matter of expediency. Once the shooting was over all the earth turned at once to the job of putting it out. You know that."

"Nope," he replied. "It worked—as did the others at Hiroshima, Nagasaki, and two at Bikini Atoll."

"Hiro—and what was at Bikini Atoll?" demanded the girl.

"Tests—Operation Crossroads."

"*Tests!*" exploded Virginia. "And none of them started atomic fires in the earth itself?"

"Nope."

"Then you tell me what happened?"

"I don't know."

"You're not psycho?" asked Virginia.

"Not that I know of," he replied with a chuckle. "Though—as Pontius Pilate is credited with having said—'What is truth?'"

"Hmmm. I cannot deny your right to state truth as you see it, Bronson, but be it remembered that practically every human born since the atomic fire is a mutation of some sort or another."

"So what does that make me?"

"You might be some sort of brain mutation—don't ask what kind—one who does not recognize the truth."

"All I know is what I read in the papers, what I see in the moving pictures, and how I feel at the moment. Also, I am no mutation. I was exactly one year old when Alamogordo took place, even supposing that it did take off with radiations that might have mutated the germ plasm."

"Well, it did."

"According to you it did," replied Bronson.

"May I repeat your own statement to yourself?" she told him. "All I know—et cetera."

"Okay," he said. "And granting that our separate tales are true, then what?"

Virginia mentioned a few items of history. Both then got their own history books and started to compare closely. They agreed on everything up to the moment of the atomic bomb at Alamogordo.

And at that moment, the histories diverged.

"Nature," said Ed Bronson, "must have been perplexed. So she took both roadways. One in which the earth is engulfed with atomic flame and one in which the thing worked."

"What do we do next?" asked Virginia.

"We get in touch with the respective authorities of our worlds," said Bronson. "Alone we can do little. Together we can do something to aid you."

"Tomorrow night at seven, then?" asked Virginia.

"Right."

The contact was broken.

"And there," said Peter Moray, "is our answer!"

Chapter III
Earth Three

Harry Maddox turned from his laboratory table as the tall, dark man entered. Maddox greeted the taller man obsequiously, but the other's reply was curt.

"They've done it, you say?" asked Kingston.

"They've done it," replied Maddox gloatingly.

"That proves it then," replied Kingston with interest. "Though it has always been a common enough theory."

"Within the past thirty-six hours," said Maddox, "there have been two transmissions. The latter one is now going on. Want to hear it?"

"Not particularly," replied Kingston. "It will be recorded for my leisure."

"Yes," nodded Maddox. His nod was toward a rather attractive girl, who was riding herd on a large wire recorder. From time to time she would reach out and adjust the volume of the recording. Over long blond hair she wore earphones to monitor the conversation directly. Kingston made a mental note that he could trust Maddox to adorn his laboratory and workshop with the most attractive human decor that he could find.

Instead of commenting on this he smiled in amusement and continued to speak. "Rather dramatic, isn't it?"

Maddox nodded. "Thirty years to the moment. That Alamogordo affair had three possibilities. It could either have gone off normally—it could have started an atomic fire in the earth—or it could have fizzled. And so, thirty years later, the three temporal possibilities are meeting."

"No, my dear Maddox," said Kingston with the air of a savant correcting a student who was not too careful of his facts. "Just two of them. We sit by— remember?"

"I know," said Maddox, rebuffed.

"Remember—and never for a moment forget—that the possibility of the Alamogordo bomb starting an atomic fire in the earth was a remote possibility. That means that the tensors which maintain that line of temporal advancement are very shaky.

"Time, you know, consists of following the Laws of Least Reaction, which simply means that in any reaction wherein a number of possibilities occur, that which will happen with the least energy will take place. This is statistically true, and need not hold for specific instances.

"Now," Kingston went on, enjoying his role of lecturer even though Maddox fiddled impatiently because he knew it all beforehand—and besides, the blonde was half-listening, though alert on her recording job. "Be it always remembered that the chances of the Alamogordo Bomb being a fizzle were as remote as the other case.

"Ergo, Maddox, our own world hangs on a slender thread of reality. We have as much need to escape from this time-slot as they whose earth is burning with atomic fire. For only in the time-slot where the Alamogordo Bomb behaved according to principle are the time-tensors heavy enough to maintain it."

"Yes, your Excellency," replied Maddox.

Kingston nodded. "You are a lucky fellow, Maddox. I came as soon as I could get away. I shall remain here until we can go through and take over."

"Sir, a question." Maddox knew that he must use deference at least until Kingston climbed down from his tall horse. "What happens when, as and if they start an atomic fire in Earth One?"

"They cannot, save by sheer chance of almost impossible mathematical odds," said Kingston. "Besides, they hope to move in—or will as soon as they learn the truth. No man burns the home he hopes to own in the near future."

"But what will happen?" asked Maddox. "That expectation is far too deep for me to follow."

"Men—all men—are inclined to feel sorry for the trapped," said Kingston. "In some cultures their sorrow is shown by killing the trapped to remove them from their misery. In other cultures, the trapped are aided even though they may eventually turn against their liberators. Once the truth is known to both worlds, those who are in Earth One will be moved to aid the trapped ones in Earth Two.

"We shall aid them as we did before by transmitting to Earth One more samples of the space-resonant radioisotope to contaminate their scientific works. There will be a gaudy search for them once the truth is known, you know. Anyway, those on Earth One will undoubtedly admit the trapped ones from Earth Two."

Maddox shrugged. "No dice, yet."

"Don't be stupid. Those on Earth Two are a race faced with death. They'll send through their mutants, their death-dealing types first. That will decimate Earth One and leave Earth One in the hands of Earth Two. Follow?"

"So far, yes. But where do we come in?"

"We come in shortly. Ninety percent of those remaining on Earth Two are mutants from the atomic fire or considerably older than thirty. The ninety are almost certain to be—if not sterile—then not cross-fertile with the rest of the mutant race. Each will have gone mutant in some fashion different from his fellow.

"All we need do then is to sit and wait until the race dies out—another thirty or forty years. Or, better, depending on the circumstances following the eventual battle, we go to war. We shall win, for our people have not lost much. At any rate we're permitting Earth Two to do our cleaning-up for us."

"Unless—" began Maddox, then paused. He knew that if he advanced a theory unasked it would be scorned. However, were he to make some leading statement and then disavow it unuttered Kingston would demand that he complete it whether he thought it right or wrong.

Kingston did, which was an excellent proof of the theory that it is a good thing to know the nature of your fellow man. "Unless what?" demanded Kingston.

"It was but an idle thought. Who fights more fiercely—he who has lost his home and fights for another or he who protects himself from the one who would dispossess him?"

Kingston laughed nastily. "Little difference," he said. "This is rigged so that no matter what, a fight will ensue. It is always easy to lick the survivor of a tough battle."

Maddox shrugged. "Just remember that you're not fighting aliens, but you—our—own kind!"

Kingston nodded. "That," he said succinctly, "is why I know them so well."

Cauldron looked at his watch. "Two hours," he said. "Time enough?"

Virginia looked concerned. "He didn't state whether he'd been asleep lately," she said.

"Unless he's a complete screwball, he'll work days and sleep nights," observed Moray. "Even supposing he works at home, he'll be arising about noon at the latest and hitting the hay about three-odd. Excepting when something was really in the fire like this receiver of his. I predict that he hit the sheets after we closed and is now pounding the pillow at a fine rate of speed."

Virginia smiled uncertainly, turning back from her communicating equipment. "He doesn't answer," she said.

"Can you locate his phosphor?" demanded Cauldron.

"I have."

"Then try," snapped Moray. "Aid! Help!" he sneered, "We're in the way of losing our very lives, and what we need, we take!"

Cauldron nodded. "Moray—you first. If Bronson is still in evidence clip him. If not we'll go ahead and do whatever is necessary. We can't take too long. After all—"

Moray nodded. "Ready, Virginia?"

"Ready."

Virginia worked over another bit of equipment in her laboratory. Moray walked over easily, smoking a last cigarette leisurely until Virginia turned to him.

"The focal volumes are resonant," she said. Then Moray seated himself in the chair before the equipment and, as Virginia started the machine, it began to transmit Pete Moray from one world to the other.

It was not especially spectacular. No flashing lights or flowing aurae of color. Moray's body, still breathing, still living, began to be less solid. At one time Moray lit another cigarette.

A bit of the cigarette smoke entered Ed Bronson's laboratory. The amount was that percentage of the transmission that had been accomplished.

There, before the big kinescope tube in Bronson's laboratory, the air was beginning to show the vague outlines of a figure, seated on a chair. This figure thickened gradually as the random atoms in Moray's body passed over.

A half hour passed and Virginia told Cauldron that the transmission should be about half complete. Moray's body could be seen through faintly—not that any of the internal organs were visible but as if he were a wraith.

Then the halfway point came. The floor in Bronson's laboratory was lower than the floor in Virginia Carlson's laboratory—with respect to their transmitters and receivers—and Moray and his chair dropped several feet on both sides. Moray seemed to be unmindful of the fact that the hard floor of Virginia's laboratory was about where his stomach was.

A half hour later, there was little of Moray left on Earth Two. Most of him was on Earth One!

As the final molecules came through the space resonator Moray heard a noise. Frantic, he turned to see but could do nothing until the last of him was complete. The noise resolved itself to footsteps, and then the door opened and Ed Bronson strode in.

"Smoke—" he mumbled sleepily, then, "—who the heck are you!"

Moray was complete. He leaped to his feet and clipped Bronson viciously with the side of his hand. Bronson dropped, stunned, dazed, but not unconscious. Deftly, Moray found a roll of tape, bound Bronson's ankles and wrists, slapped a bit of tape across his mouth.

"Aid?" sneered Moray. "Promise us aid, all right. Fifty years will pass while the idea is being thrashed out in Congress or in whatever international organization there is here. Behave, Bronson, and you'll live. Help us— understand? If you don't it's—" Moray drew a forefinger across his throat.

Another figure started to form—vague and indistinct—and Moray lifted the taped man across his shoulders, carried him upstairs, dumped him across his bed and left him there.

When he returned to the laboratory, Virginia was beginning to solidify. Moray seated himself and waited, smoking Bronson's cigarettes and fortifying himself with a drink of Bronson's liquor. Moray smiled, but his humor was bitter.

How to marshal an army? It took an hour to get one person through—to pass the six or seven million still living in Earth Three would at this rate take six or seven million hours—a mere eight hundred years if you didn't bother with the extra leap-year days or take Christmas off.

Time passed slowly and it was the full hour before Virginia came through completely and arose from her chair.

"Collect Bronson or kill him?" she asked.

"I should have killed him," said Moray.

"Not at all," replied Virginia. "Even though this is quite similar to our world remember that thirty years of time separate us—and thirty years each of divergent development. We need someone to show us our way around."

Moray shrugged. "He might guess about this factor?"

Virginia shook her head. "No," she said with finality. "He's just beginning to think about the space resonator. Look at that pile of haywire junk! He's downright dumbfounded at the idea of communicating over a lump of electron-bombarded radioisotopic compound.

"To consider the transmission of matter from one volume of focus to another is an idea beyond concept. And—no doubt—radioisotopes aren't dished out as easily here as they are back there."

"Here, there, whither?" grinned Moray. "Let's call this Earth One because it is going to be here long after Earth Two has dissolved in atomic flame."

"Okay. So we've got this station first. We've got to get enough radioisotopic phosphor passed around Earth One to make wholesale passage possible. You run this station, Moray, and I'll stand by to act as a front."

Moray looked at Virginia closely. Slender, blonde and possessed of an ethereal and almost violent beauty, her personality and looks could and would forestall much idle questioning. He nodded.

"You keep out of sight of Friend Bronson," he said. "It might be handy to have you for a—a face card."

Virginia grinned....

Ed Bronson had a splitting headache and a crying pain in every muscle. He had been lying motionless. It was all he could do against the adhesive-taping job done by Peter Moray. His tongue was thick and furry and his very soul cried for water. He could make no sound for the tape covered his mouth.

Angrily, and resentfully, Bronson's temper flared. He set his muscles against the tape about his wrists and strained. He tried the tape about his ankles. Both were wound many times with the heavy tape which would not be torn.

A twisting strain succeeded only in abrading his skin until the flesh was raw and bleeding. With fading hope he prayed that the blood would soften the tape and thought about rubbing himself raw even more so that the further flow of blood might aid.

He gave that up when he saw that the tape was of the waterproof variety. All the soaking in the world would do little good.

He rolled from the bed onto the floor, easing the thud by dropping taped feet first and then angling to knees, turning to land on his buttocks and then unfolding as gently as he knew how. He made it with no undue effort. Then he rolled across the floor to the door and, turning, he caught the hinge-butt under the tape at his wrists where tape and wrists made a small triangle.

After many minutes, Bronson succeeded in weakening the tape and then, hooking the tape firmly over the hinge, he tore it loose. To remove the tape from his mouth and from his ankles was but a moment's work and then Ed Bronson was free to act!

Quietly, he dressed. Then, using the utmost stealth, he stole down the stairs and out onto the street. It was midmorning.

Nodding amicably to Lewis McManner, who scowled back across the street, Ed Bronson headed for police headquarters.

Chapter IV
"What Fools—"

Ed Bronson thought it out on his way to the police station. Man was an impossible mixture of altruism and selfishness. Man was inclined to give freely to those who were needy—but would fight like fury to withhold the very smallest of his possessions from the avaricious grasp of those who would wrest them from him by force.

As a world requiring pity, aid and mercy, every effort would be bent towards that end, even to the job of making room for them in an already crowded world. But they had entered like bank robbers or claim jumpers. Their own world lost, they intended to abandon it, pirating any other world they could.

The brotherhood of man collapsed at that point and became a brotherhood of hate. Tolerance and mercy and willingness to offer succor must be forgotten when the needy become vicious. Biting the hand that feeds is an old platitude which still holds true.

So Ed Bronson knew that, regardless of their wretched situation, they must be stopped. This was invasion with capital letters. Even though many of them must be direct descendants of people in this world, invasion meant war! Even worse than civil war was the brother against brother, man against man, war of survival.

They—and Ed Bronson paused. 'They' was an indefinite term. 'They' should have some nomenclature for purposes of identification. Were the invasion from another planet, 'they' would have a name.

Were it merely an earthly war, country against country or political clan against political clan, both sides would have names. But here was a case where it would be one earth, one world, against another world—identical save for a trick in time that had split them apart.

Bronson needed a name and he needed it quickly. He reasoned and came to the conclusion that the 'other world' should be called Earth Two because it was not long for living. Once it was destroyed by its own fire this world would revert to being '*the*' earth. Until such a time as differentiation became unnecessary he would call the two worlds Earth One and Earth Two.

Thus, independently, did the people of three almost identical earths arrive at the same conclusion. Earth One was the original, where the Alamogordo Experiment had been successful. Earth Two was where the million-to-one chance of starting an all-consuming atomic fire had actually happened. Earth Three was where the Alamogordo Experiment had failed.

Ed Bronson and the folk from Earth Two were still to learn of Earth Three and it was only sheer reasoning that made all three systems of nomenclature congruent.

So by the time Ed Bronson located the police department he was prepared to give a coherent story. He asked for the captain in charge.

"Cap'n Norris is busy," grumped the desk sergeant. "What's the matter?"

"My home is being invaded and—"

"Well, you don't need the captain for that," snapped the sergeant. "Joe! Eddie! Get the wagon and go with this here—what's your name, mister?—and see that the guys that broke into his place are canned!"

"I'm Ed Bronson," explained Ed. "But—"

"That's all right," grunted the sergeant. "Joe and Eddie'll take care of you!"

"But you don't understand," said Ed patiently. "These are invaders from another world."

"Invaders from—what?" asked the sergeant, doing a double take.

"They're just the beginning," said Ed. "If you manage to grab them others will be coming."

"Eddie—Joe! Forget it. This is a Number Seven deal."

Joe and Eddie looked at Ed Bronson with an odd glint in their eyes. The sergeant looked down across the desk and said, "Now, Mr. Bronson, suppose you come with me to the captain's office and we'll talk to him."

"That's fine," said Bronson. "You see, I'm not sure of what to do about it all."

"Captain Norris will be able to help you," said the sergeant. "This way."

He came from behind his desk and led Ed Bronson to the hallway door. He opened the door and stepped back, permitting Ed to go first. Ed found himself in a short hallway and started down it uncertainly. The sergeant followed him until he reached the proper door.

"In there, Mr. Bronson," he said.

Bronson did not make particular note of the fact that the desk sergeant had at no time been with his back to Ed. He opened the door and found himself facing an elderly wise-looking man who had the appearance of having seen, heard, and experienced, either first-hand or vicariously, every item of trouble, grief and sin in the list.

"Captain Norris, this is Mr. Bronson. He has a bit of trouble. Thought you'd best hear about it."

"Sit down, Mr. Bronson, and tell me about it," replied Captain Norris easily.

"Well, sir, in the first place, I am an electronics specialist. It's—"

"A scientist of some sort, is that it?"

Ed nodded. "Most of us shy away from the name 'scientist' but that's about it," he said. "So you're a scientist?" smiled Norris.

"Yes. And I was experimenting on a bit of radioisotopic phosphor, hoping to make a better, more brilliant television picture."

"Has this all got to do with the people who are breaking into your home?" asked Norris.

"Yes. That's how they got in."

"I see. Then go ahead. No, Sergeant Foster, you stay because you may have to do something about this and it is best that you get your story first hand. It'll save time. Now, Mr. Bronson?"

"Well, under the combined forces of the magnetic field and the electronic bombardment the phosphor vibrated. I half recognized the vibration. It was like a very faint whisper in another room that you can't quite understand—but you know that someone is whispering.

"So I went to work on the phosphor and used a contact microphone on it, and got in touch with some woman, who gave her address as across the street from my home. When I went over there, I discovered that it couldn't possibly be correct. Later I refined the thing a bit and learned that her name was Carlson. Then I built a means of talking back to her, and I learned that she was not on this world at all. It was—"

"Not on this earth—but talking American?" demanded Norris.

"Yes."

"Do go on," said Captain Norris, putting down his pipe and leaning forward a bit.

"Well, you see, Captain Norris, there were some of the Manhattan Project physicists who believed that there was a chance that the atomic explosion might be strong enough to start a fission train in the earth itself. In other words, they were afraid of setting the earth on fire atomically. This was a possibility, and it seems that we now have two worlds, each following the natural chain of events pursuant to the two different possibilities."

"Very interesting, Mr. Bronson. Please go on. There must be more."

"After learning this, we decided to do what we could to alleviate the difficulty. I went to bed. In the night—or rather while I was asleep, they used some means or other to pass through from one world to the other and one of them clipped me and taped me up. He told me that they were going to move in on us—to displace us. I escaped and came here. Something must be done!"

"Indeed! Something must be done indeed," replied Captain Norris.

Bronson took a deep breath, and said, "I'm glad that I had this chance. It was a heavy weight on my mind, knowing that this was happening and I was the only one in the whole world that knew the truth."

Captain Norris nodded. "I trust that you are feeling all right now?"

"Of course."

"We'd better get you to a doctor, Mr. Bronson. Those wrists look inflamed."

Bronson looked down at them. "Now that this affair is in the hands of authority," he said, "I think I can take time off to see a doctor."

"We'll take you to our doctor," said Captain Norris.

"I have my own," said Bronson.

"We—insist!"

"But—"

Norris smiled genially. "You'll like our doctor," he said. "He's such a nice congenial fellow. Everybody likes him. Now—"

"What is this?" demanded Bronson.

"Take it easy," said the captain, "it's just routine. Everybody who gets hurt in the course of committing a crime or being victimized in such is always treated by the official medical department. Just a matter of establishing legal medical evidence, that's all. Now relax, Mr. Bronson, and come along. I'll have the boys take you to the hospital."

"Hos—?"

"Routine. The doctor works for us, Mr. Bronson. Therefore he has no office hours. Logical?"

Joe and Eddie treated Ed Bronson to a wild ride through the city streets with the siren on full. They slid to a stop in front of a squat, dirty limestone building and they escorted him in—convoyed him in, to be exact, for one went in front and one followed up the rear.

"I am Doctor Mason," said a white-clad man, meeting them in the corridor of the building. "Captain Norris told me you'd be coming."

"Just abraded skin, doctor," said Ed, showing the doctor his wrists.

"We'll take care of that instanter," smiled Doctor Mason. "Meanwhile, what's this tale you were telling Norris? Something about hearing voices? Threatening voices?"

Bronson recoiled a bit.

"Now, relax," said Mason.

"Do you think I'm crazy?" asked Bronson sharply.

"Of course not. You're not crazy, my boy. Just tell me—"

"You—"

"My friend, the symptoms of paranoia are simple and easy to determine. The hushed voices, in the earlier stages, merely talk about the victim. In a later stage the voices threaten. In still a later state the hushed voices take physical being and all too often it is someone entirely innocent of any malice.

"Now this tale of people from another world, Mr. Bronson, must be faced for what it is. You are not crazy, my boy. Merely ill—no worse than a bad cold or influenza, for instance. But you are ill and you must be treated."

"Treated?" exploded Bronson angrily. "Treated—for an imagined mental ailment when the earth itself is in danger of being invaded?"

"The earth is not in danger," said the psychiatrist firmly. "And—"

"I will not be—"

"Violent, too," said Mason with a solemn shake of his head. "Normally, we try to gain the patient's confidence. But in advanced cases of paranoia, they will resent even altruism. Everything is suspected of plot. Now, Mr. Bronson, whether you believe that this is for your own good or not, you're coming with me. Will you come quietly or shall I have some orderlies bring you?"

Bronson shook his head and turned to go. He walked into the waiting arms of Joe and Eddie, who subdued him easily because they were well trained in the art of handling men. Mason waved them on, and Bronson walked with both arms in hammerlock behind him. He could either walk or have both arms dislocated at the shoulder.

Mason spoke to the policemen. "The thing that makes psychiatry tough is that the patient likes himself the way he is—just as all men do, really—and resents bitterly any suggestion that his personality be changed."

"What do you intend to do?" asked Joe.

"Electro-therapy," said the doctor in a decisive tone.

Bronson writhed in both physical and mental anguish. He, the only man on earth that realized the danger, being dog-walked into a cell—accused of the crime of warning the earth of its fate! Outnumbered, overpowered and disbelieved!

Chapter V
Head Start

Leader Kingston shook his head. "Bronson is dangerous to us," he said.

Maddox nodded. "If his tale is believed Earth One will arm against invasion."

"Correct. Properly to save us trouble the invasion must take place against small armed odds. Otherwise, instead of our finding a world decimated and wearied by war, we'll find a world with its wits sharpened and its anger high."

Maddox turned the focus knob to readjust the image that had fuzzed a bit because of a varying line voltage. He pointed to Bronson's image, struggling against the policemen.

"He's in a fix right now," he said.

Kingston nodded dubiously. "But he'll not remain there," he said. "Bronson is suspected of being paranoid right now. Any man coming to high authority with such an unbelievable tale of alien entities or time-divided worlds would be suspected of insanity. But before anybody tries to cure him, they will give him their most extensive tests to prove or disprove his sanity.

"It is a fundamental principle that no man need be subjected to treatments or cure that needs them not. It is a violation of human integrity to attempt to cure a man of delusions who has no instability. Therefore they will apply the last word in checks and tests and discover that Bronson is not insane.

"Once they discover his stability they will admit the shadow of a doubt. Only the completely insane will not admit their error or possibility of error. An honestly sane man will admit—however grudgingly—the possibility of anything, even to alien entities and split time-continua."

"Then—?"

"Then let them listen but once to his flanged-up space resonator. His is a fine spectacle, you admit—about as neat and as efficient as the First Radio Receiver. On such, many people are making many transmissions of all sorts. Obviously, Maddox, the state of the art is higher than the technical efficiency of Bronson's gadget which to men of science will mean that there is something to Bronson's story. Follow?"

Maddox nodded. "The men who know will have sufficient knowledge to evaluate the negative evidence. They know of no such technique."

"Exactly," nodded Kingston. "Precisely. This we must stop!"

"This we can stop," said Maddox.

"How?" demanded Kingston sharply.

Maddox made a wry grin. "Watch," he said. He turned to the kinescope screen once more and watched Ed Bronson prowling the lonely cell....

For the thirtieth time, Ed Bronson paced his tiny cell. It was hopeless. Everything mobile was too large and soft to use as tool or weapon—for either egress or self-destruction. His clothing had been removed forcibly and Ed Bronson seethed angrily, dressed in only his skin.

He realized that he had been a fool. Had he been less violent he might not be so well incarcerated. He should have known that no amount of physical struggle would get him anything. After all he had striven against greater numbers of men who were all trained in the art of handling men possessed of the strength of the insane.

Bronson had only the strength of the indignant, which was far from the unreasonable power of the insane. With the use of a small amount of foresight, Ed Bronson knew that he might have been in a room less bare, perhaps one in which the door had not been bolted, barred and locked.

Bronson, it must be told, was not aware of the fact that the men who held him were also used to prisoners possessed of the cunning of the insane. No amount of cajolery, honest protest, supine acquiescence or willing aid would have made them do other than lock, bolt and bar his door.

What Bronson needed was a friend....

Maddox smiled with grim humor. "We cannot silence him now."

Kingston nodded, his face clearing of its slight frown. "Good man," he breathed.

"Nor," said Maddox, looking at the cell depicted on the kinescope tube, "can we aid him to escape."

"To kill him inside of that room would most certainly prove to them that enough of his tale is true to make them suspicious. Even to open that room and let him out will prove to them that there is more than the agency of a single man at work."

"In other, terser words," grunted Maddox, "he has placed himself in a position where he has life insurance—only in the name of Earth Three."

"And you see to it that he stays alive, suspect and helpless!" snapped Kingston.

"That I shall do," nodded Maddox. "That I shall do!"

"Unless, of course, he is threatened by death with both killer and motive indigenous—or apparently so—to Earth One."

Peter Moray turned to Virginia Carlson and shook his head. "Won't work," he said.

"Why not?" she asked.

Moray explained. His explanation was almost identical to that of Kingston and Maddox. To hurl a man into an asylum for hallucination is all well and good. To protect society, for any number of reasons all directed at the protection of society, from the maniac or to protect the maniac from society is sound.

Yet no man can be incarcerated very long if he is sane and wants to get out. It is as difficult for a sane man to fake insanity as it is for an insane man to fake insanity.

"So what do we do now?" asked Virginia.

"We should have eliminated him at once," snapped Moray. "Confound it, I was sleeping. I thought he might be useful."

"You were wrong," she said. "It seems to me that we might as well give him the works. I'll go down and see that he is taken care of."

Peter Moray nodded. Bronson had seen Moray but had never seen Virginia. In fact, Bronson knew only Virginia's last name. That was a help. Also, Virginia was a very good looking young woman and the power of a beautiful woman who speaks with certainty is great. She was also a capable calculator and could plan her campaign as she went along. Moray nodded, and Virginia headed for the asylum.

In her handbag, Virginia carried a small automatic. Bronson was a threat. The threat must be eliminated. The lover's quarrel perhaps or, better, he was in the asylum for paranoia. Why not have him attack her? Self-defense is a good alibi and her story would be strengthened by the doctor's decision. She smiled cryptically.

Supposing she were convicted of murder in the first degree and sentenced to the gas chamber? By the time the trial came to its end, the invasion would be ready and the first act of the men of Earth Two would be to rescue Virginia from her cell. She had everything to gain, nothing to lose by acting—and there was an entire world dependent upon her.

Confidently Virginia opened the door of Bronson's house and headed down the street. It was her first venture outside along the ways of Earth One.

In the morning, from her home, there were two lights in the sky, one a disc rising in the east, one a blinding glare that rendered the disc ineffective. Albuquerque never really knew night nor had it during the course of Virginia Carlson's life. Here, however, there was but the shining sun and Virginia found the streets a bit sheltered, shadowed, compared to the streets of her home.

But—the thought came to her—this was her home! She walked along the same street as the one she lived on. She looked across the street from Bronson's front steps and saw her own number there. It was a different house but none the less it was her number. It was sandwiched between two other houses whose outlines and architecture she recognized.

The street light was there, recognizable, though this one was not the remaining remnant of the pre-Alamogordo era. The one in her Albuquerque had not been used in the course of her life, though it had not been removed.

The street-car line was still on the next corner, and the cars that ran might have been the same—could they have been? Interested, Virginia waited until one came along and, though she could not be certain, it seemed the same.

It was a matter of interest to find out whether the same cars plied the same tracks in two different time streams. This seemed at once paradoxical and quite possible, for Virginia had seen both her own street address with a new house on the location, and the houses on either side which were older than Alamogordo and recognizable.

Virginia walked on slowly, a number of things running through her mind. Even though the city seemed the same, there was quite a difference. The population was thick here, not thinned out by radiation-sterility. The people were smiling and unafraid. On no face was that look of stark wonder and fear that never left the faces of the people of Earth Two even though they had been born and bred under the blinding light of the Alamogordo Blow-up.

Nor were there the mutants.

That was what made the most difference. In her life and counted among her friends were strange biological forms, often unhuman. There was, for instance, a fellow called Thomas Lincoln whose eyes grew on stalks and was quite a man at work on large machinery because he could see deep within the machine without having to rely on mirrors or the sense of touch.

His eyes, when extended, could either assume the proper distance for perspective, could narrow or widen the angle of perspective—and his mind, trained over the years, made due allowance so that he knew and accepted these differences.

There was Greene, the man whose hands had a palm on either side and whose fingers could bend to make a fist on either the inside or the outside of the arm. This might seem good, but it presented a lack of firmness. Greene's hands were far weaker than Harrison's, whose hands had but three fingers with twin thumbs on either side, making the hand symmetrical.

Her girl-friend, Edna, secreted pure metal instead of pigment and her skin and hair had a metallic sheen that was rather beautiful. In a strong light, Edna's skin and hair were almost luminous, like iridescent paint. There was the fellow that lived on the corner—Virginia never knew his name—who had a double knee and elbow. This made for physical instability.

There were others. Some were interesting from functional standpoints, some were interesting from banal standpoints. Others were just horrible and many were viciously dangerous. But many of them were her friends. Virginia had grown up without one iota of prejudice regarding the shape of a man's body, the color of his skin, or the nationality of his father. For in a life where few men were as simply mutated as to have a mere skin coloration, all of the former prejudices were so minor in the face of the acceptance of the more violent differences that to accept the latter meant complete disregard of the former.

This world contrasted sharply with Virginia's world. To see people walking freely in the streets, pursuing their normal life, was puzzling. Virginia, born in the glare of Alamogordo, under a culture that had devoted itself completely to one main idea or to the secondary or tertiary support of those who pursued that idea, this freedom was inexplicable.

In Virginia's world, there were two classes of people—those who worked directly on the problem of saving their world in one way or another and those who worked to support those who worked on the problem. Farmers produced so much, by law. Book dealers sold so many kinds of books, produced by printers and publishers who did exactly what was needed and no more. Entertainment and relaxation was far from spontaneous.

People did not collect at random and throw a party on the spur of the moment nor could one decide to go out and buy a magazine and read it instead of cleaning out the basement. Though it was admitted as such, it was an emergency dictatorship, with the Alamogordo Blow-up as main dictator. Regulation was the order of the years.

Earth One was, to Virginia, completely unregulated. Women walked along the streets idly, looking in windows and smiling at men. The sign "Bar" intrigued Virginia. She was no stranger to the potable qualities of alcohol, but the concept of an establishment directed at the sole idea of selling drinks had not occurred to her.

This—recall—was Virginia's first experience in living in a world not harassed by fear.

She paused at a window showing an assortment of dresses on well-made forms. In her world, Virginia was a good-looking woman and dressed as well as the next.

In contrast to a world where much time and energy was directed at luxury instead of the sheer, vicious necessity driven of hope and despair— in a world where the accolade of young womanhood is to be permitted her first trip to mother's beauty salon and thereafter make obeisance regularly— Virginia, a beauty in her own world, knew that here she was as conspicuous as a tall telephone pole in a snowbound prairie.

She knew because the window before which she stood reflected her own hand-made dress against the luxurious mannequin inside the window.

Moray had been correct in his assumption that a beautiful woman could get away with more than a plain one. His only mistake was in not judging alien demands for grooming. And yet it was not a true mistake. It was rooted in sheer ignorance.

Virginia wondered. Money? Coinage does not change very often. But the few coins she had in her bag would not cover the two figures to the left of the decimal point—iffing and providing that they were still good.

There was, on her right hand, her mother's diamond. On her left wrist was a wristwatch of quite ancient vintage—Virginia automatically called it "Pre-Blast"—which might bring a few dollars.

Virginia turned from the window and went across the street to a pawnshop. She emerged with a handful of greenbacks, re-crossed the street and entered the ladies' shop. With satisfaction Virginia noted a beautician's place next door and, though rather questioning of the nefarious arts that might go on behind the curtains, Virginia was determined to compete with her contemporary girl-friends on an even basis—perhaps with a fair head start!

Chapter VI
Sprung by the Foe

John Cauldron made contact with Peter Moray shortly after Virginia had gone. Moray, busy with the details at hand, had not given much time to thinking out the course of the future. Besides, it was Moray's business to act upon orders from above. His was not the planner's lot.

"What's cooking?" he asked Cauldron.

"We're putting on a security silence on the space resonators," replied Cauldron.

"Why?"

"Whether they think Bronson insane or not, whether he lives or dies, we must see that there are as many bits of radioisotopic phosphor in Earth One as possible."

"Yes, but—"

"Bronson may be judged insane. However, give him a chance and he will demonstrate the space resonator. If he should pick up an Earth Two broadcast or even a molecular pattern it will lend weight to his tale. On the other hand, Bronson will be given credit—sane or otherwise—for the invention of a new level of communication.

"When it becomes known that gross matter can be shipped across space with the same scientific concept people will rush madly to develop and build delivery sets."

"I get it."

"Sure," replied Cauldron. "It's easy enough. Tell Virginia—"

"She's gone already. She left to take care of Bronson."

"Oh blast! Look, Moray, how are people dressed there?"

"Why—I wouldn't know. Bronson was in pajamas when I intercepted him and it's just barely morning now. I've not really been out yet."

"You should have taken time to get Virginia fixed up as close to one of the women of this world as possible."

"Why?"

"Because she'll be less conspicuous," said Bronson. "If they get to peering into Bronson's mind they'll come to the conclusion that he isn't as mad as his tale sounds. Give them one overly-conspicuous character to look at and they will definitely begin to think loud thoughts."

"Well, why shouldn't Virginia get along?" demanded Moray.

"You're a young squirt," snapped Cauldron shortly. "You weren't around before the blow-up. You haven't the vaguest idea of how much time and hard money was spent by women on the luxury of appearing beautiful. That has been curtailed on Earth Two by necessity and emergency. But I'll bet a tall hat that they are still shelling out plenty there. Is there a telephone book handy?"

"Yeah," said Moray.

"Then crack it to the classified section and tell me how many pages there are of beauty shops, beauty salons, beauticians, or whatever they're called."

Silence ensued for several minutes and then Peter Moray returned and gave Cauldron the answer.

"You see?" replied Cauldron. "You have no idea of how life is lived when there is no cause for fear."

"So—"

"So I'd feel better if Virginia were heading for that place in something better than a hand-made dress of reclaimed cloth, a self-done hairdo and flat-heeled slippers. Besides," he chuckled wryly, "it would help her morale no end."

Harry Maddox turned from the hapless spectacle of Ed Bronson and shrugged. "He's safe," he said. "Now what?..."

"They've gone into a security silence," said Kingston. "As we expected."

"Then our friend Bronson is no longer needed?"

"Nope. They'll get along without him, now. What worries me is that the psychiatrist may get to work on Bronson long enough to establish a reasonable doubt in their minds."

"Even so," said Maddox thoughtfully, "we're stuck. Supposing we were to kill him? It's obviously impossible in that room. It is equally impossible for him to escape nor can we arrange it."

"What we need is a person who might be quite willing to murder Bronson in cold blood for the sake of murder itself—or even better, for some mundane motive."

"What about the characters from Earth Two?" suggested Maddox.

"Let's find 'em," snapped Kingston, apparently struck with an idea.

Maddox had little trouble in locating Moray. He looked in on Peter Moray for a moment, and then went in search of Virginia. Virginia, apparently, had disappeared.

It was quite impossible to search every possible place in Albuquerque for a glimpse of Virginia and, after covering the pathway to and from Bronson's cottage to the police station and thence to the police hospital, Maddox gave up and returned to Moray, who had stopped speaking to Cauldron. As Moray turned away from the equipment, the telephone rang, and he went to it, wondering.

Moray lifted the phone and said, gingerly, "Yes? This is the Brons—"

"Moray! This is Virginia. I'm going to dig Bronson out of the clink and bring him home. You hide or at least lie low. Follow?"

"Where are you?"

Virginia named an address.

Kingston snapped, "Get that address—quick. Know where it is?"

"Heck," drawled Maddox insolently, "This is the same Albuquerque. Sure I know the address."

The video screen showed a blur, and settled on the showroom of a ladies' apparel shop. Virginia was just hanging up the telephone and Maddox whistled.

"Knockout," he said succinctly.

"She got the works," grinned Kingston. "Thanks to her we can watch."

"Well," said Maddox thoughtfully, "there goes your party with murderous intent, and quite worldly too."

Kingston nodded. "That automatic in her bag isn't an unaccustomed weapon," he said thoughtfully. "And she can and will claim attack. Self defense...."

Clad in a printed silk that graced her svelte body caressingly, with the sheerest of hose, the seams of which ran die-true down from the hem of her dress to her sandal-shod, tiny feet, Virginia Carlson of Earth Two was well on her way to being the most fetching woman in three worlds. Her hair had been coiffed to perfection and her face had been made up by an expert.

Virginia looked soft and sweet and perfect. She was a sight that made men turn to watch but not to whistle because she radiated some quality that rendered the wolf-whistle a definite insult.

Then, patting the automatic confidently, Virginia turned down along the street once more and headed for the police hospital. Though she could not know it, the plane of focus of the video resonator followed her. Maddox and Kingston were watching her as she went.

"Once this is finished," thought Virginia, "I shall enjoy living like this!"

Her feet, unaccustomed to dancing, did a pointless little step. Her eyes sparkled, iris wide even in the morning sunshine, for Earth One had no eternal light in the sky to keep a dazzling brightness day and night. She pirouetted once and the sleek silk frock whirled and clung to her legs. As she stopped, the weight of the automatic in her bag hit her and reminded her of a job to be done before all this could be hers.

Bronson must be stopped—somehow!

Virginia knew how.

With a fetching smile on her face Virginia entered the police hospital and asked for the police physician. Doctor Mason came and was a bit set back by the obviously high quality of his caller.

"You're—?"

"Virginia Wells. I'm a friend of Mr. Bronson."

"Indeed? A peculiar case, Miss Wells," he observed gravely.

"Not at all," she said with a smile. "Mr. Bronson, as a hobby, has been writing fiction and we got into an argument as to whether high authority could hear a rather bizarre tale without thinking the story teller was insane. I won."

"So that's it," grunted Doctor Mason. "He sounded sincere enough to me."

Virginia shrugged shapely shoulders and hurled at him the dazzle of her smile. "After all," she said in an entrancing contralto, "he is a successful author even though he doesn't work at it one hundred percent of the time. He should be able to concoct a story that would hold water, and he should be convincing. Why, that's his business!"

"Um."

Mason left the office for a moment and came back with Bronson at his heels—dressed.

Virginia gave Bronson a warning look and then laughed at him. "Like spending the night in the clink, Ed?" she asked brightly.

"No!" he snapped.

"You needn't have," she said with a smile. "All you had to do was tell them the truth. Why, they'd have thrown Orson Welles into jail for the Martian Invasion if he hadn't been famous."

Bronson started. The Orson Welles affair had taken place a long time ago—before either of them were born, in fact. This rather glorious girl was trying to tell him something.

"Yeah," he drawled, stalling for time.

"All right, so you lost," she told him. "And now, if you don't have to stay here for playing pranks, we can go on home and write it up."

Bronson looked at Mason. Mason shrugged. "What's the pitch?" he asked. "As for me, no—we don't want you though I'd like to have you reprimanded for wasting time."

"Come to think of it, Doctor Mason, how should a man try to tell high authority of some impending form of outrageous doom?" asked Virginia.

"Why—" stammered Doctor Mason, "I—"

"Yes," snapped Bronson angrily. "Tell us!"

"Why?"

"Because," said Virginia, sweetly, "some day someone is really going to come up with invaders from outer space or some other unbelievable little item and, while the big bright brass is psychoanalyzing the discoverer, the invasion or the doom will take place."

"Why—I'm—"

"Forget it, Mason," said Bronson. Then, because he was completely unaware of his visitor's name or anything else about her save that she knew something that prompted her to aid him, Bronson turned to the girl and held out an elbow.

"May I escort you home, Madame Pompadour?"

Virginia smiled at him with exaggerated enticement. "Only if you want to be Benjamin Franklin, dear."

Doctor Mason stood up and hurled the door open angrily. "Get the devil out of here!" he snapped. He was still looking for a fine vocabulary when they left. Once outside and on the street beyond, Ed Bronson paused.

"Now," he said seriously, "what in the name of eternal sin is this?"

"I had to get you out of there," she said. "I'm glad you are sharp enough to follow suit."

"You can be glad that Mason did not choose to question me about you," snapped Bronson. "I'd have denied you deeply."

"All a part of your tale to convince," she smiled. "I'd have forced it into the open—forced Mason to let us meet. Then we'd make out."

"Fine, fine," he said with a bitter grin. "Just tell me what the score is right now."

"I happen to know that you are right," she told him.

"But—"

She nodded. She explained at length that she had been tinkering in her cellar and had come in with something that had permitted her to hear his half of the initial discussion with the girl named Carlson.

She paused at that point and grinned at him. "Just to keep the record clear," she said, "I'm Virginia Wells."

"Well, Miss Wells, I'm grateful. But what does a girl like you find interesting in tinkering in the cellar?"

"You call me Virginia like everybody else," she told him. "As for tinkering in the cellars, when has a woman's appeal anything to do with the liking for science—and furthermore I might even resent the phrase 'like you' that was hurled at me. Do you think anybody that looks like this must necessarily be completely vacant above the ears?"

Bronson smiled. "Not every girl," he said with a sour smile. "But the percentage assays high."

Virginia took a deep breath. Thin though her story was, he'd accepted it for the nonce.

"Where do we go from here?" he asked. "I want to reason this thing out."

Virginia smiled tolerantly. "My equipment isn't very good," she said. "I'd like to see yours."

Bronson smiled. For hours he had been itching to show someone the equipment and this was his chance. He was going to take the opportunity regardless of where the chance came. Virginia had known that too!

The girl tucked a slender hand into the crook of his elbow. "Let's go," she said with a bright smile.

Bronson nodded and they started toward his home.

He walked easily, she thought, neither too fast nor too slowly. His stride seemed to coincide with hers so that the periods of out-of-step walking were minimized. They were not nonexistent, for Ed Bronson was a tall, long-legged man and, though Virginia's legs were long and slender, she was not so tall as Ed Bronson by seven inches.

"I might suggest," said Bronson thoughtfully, "that we can do a bit of talking while we collect us some lunch. Me—I'm hungry."

Virginia paused. Visiting a restaurant was another thing that was seldom done on Earth Two, excepting by those who found it essential. This she viewed as another luxury and she wanted to try it. On the other hand, she had too thin a story prepared regarding her 'experiments' with the space-resonant crystals of radioisotopic phosphor, of her listening to Bronson and his subsequent rescue from the asylum.

Yet—Virginia shrugged slightly—she could probably handle this. Besides, she could learn more of Earth One were she to visit with Bronson.

Virginia nodded and smiled at him. Bronson paused in mid-stride and turned toward a small restaurant he knew. Inwardly he chuckled to himself. It was not always that a woman rescuer, fellow scientist and friend-indeed was so very delectable. Bronson was proud to have such a woman in his company.

Chapter VII
Transfer Arranged

The automatic computer in the laboratory of atomic physics at the New Mexico University on Earth Three was a vast thing that encompassed many acres of wiring, tubes and memory-storage circuits.

It had been working silently—save for an occasional click—for an hour, which was a pointed commentary on the depth of the problem presented to it, since its usual time of operation was startling in its brevity. It was, without a doubt, the great-great-grandfather of all automatic computers and even it was forced to mull over the problem.

Leader Kingston and Harry Maddox lounged before the massive control board, smoking and watching Virginia and Bronson on a small remote-presentation kinescope.

Finally the machine emitted a series of typewriter-like clicks and a sheet of paper emerged from the slot. It bore a complex equation that Maddox took and pored over.

Kingston waited quietly, for he knew that Maddox was far more capable than he at interpreting the equations. Any interference would interrupt Maddox, ruin his train of thought and require more time in the long run.

Finally Maddox looked up and smiled.

"It seems so," he said.

"There is no definite proof?" demanded Kingston.

"Time and the future are both based upon the laws of probability," replied Maddox. "That these three worlds do exist side by side by side in time is certain—that they might have existed at any time before they did start was a matter of probability. Anything is probable, you know. That we live is a most certain probability, yet that we will continue to live is less certain."

"You're talking in circles," snapped Kingston. "Get to the point!"

"Sorry, I must sound vague. You see, Leader, I've been thinking about this for some time and therefore I am inclined to think over the well-worn thought-trails swiftly and in considerable elision. However, according to this equation, the fact is this. The spatial continuum is strained by the unnatural presence of three congruent pathways through the present time.

"As we know, only the most probable of these will continue to exist. That—unfortunately—is Earth One. The Alamogordo experiment on Earth One was the most probable, of course. Obviously Earth Two is destined to die soon, leaving but Earths One and Three.

"But," continued Maddox thoughtfully, "we have posed the problem and the machine here reasons that we are correct."

"Then we need not undergo all the strife in order to survive!"

"Obviously not. Once the pathways through time are no longer strained by multiple existences the strain will cease. In other words, once we—Earth Three—are the only true survivor the strain will cease and there will be no fear of our demise."

"Then all we need do is to eliminate One and Two—and then," Kingston grinned, "Earth Three becomes the only one?"

"Three becomes One," nodded Maddox. "Now—"

"Now we figure out a means of destroying Earth One utterly."

"Simple," said Maddox. "All we need do is to rotate a bit of the core of the Alamogordo Blow-up from Earth Two to Earth One."

"Might be less simple than we think," said Kingston. "Remember that the fission train in the earth itself is indigenous to Earth Two. Since it did not happen on Earth One is there any reason to suppose that the earth of Earth One will support an atomic fire?"

Maddox shook his head. "When the bomb was tried—I nearly said 'went off' but it didn't here—the temporal strain broke into three paths," said Maddox. "The three important possibilities took place—obviously because there was a huge question as to which of the three possibilities would emerge as the successful outcome of the affair."

"I'm no believer in the Great Destiny," said Kingston.

"Nor am I," said Maddox. "Yet it is true that the most fit do survive. Obviously, Earth Two and its atomic fire is far from the most fit. Earth One has dropped into a lulled luxury-loving place where the serious facets of life are ignored. They are unprepared to enter any form of strife to survive. We—Earth Three—have developed ourselves and our science greatly and in any strife we are best fitted to survive!"

"All right, it sounds logical," snapped Kingston. "But how do we prove it without arousing suspicion?"

"We can rotate a bit of the core of the Earth Two atomic fire to this earth," said Maddox. "Once we establish the atomically-inflammable qualities of Earth Three, we can safely assume that Earth One will be the same. Remember," said Maddox with a grin, "on Earth Three the Alamogordo Bomb was a dud—it didn't even fire!"

"And then what?" sneered Kingston. "It seems to me that your suggestion is the beginning of the end."

"Not at all. Once we establish the possibility beyond a doubt, we can so very easily rotate the hunk of atomic fire back into Earth Two again."

Kingston thought for a moment. Then he nodded. "We must move lightning fast," he said sharply. "Because I will hazard a bet that Earth Two considered the idea of getting rid of their atomic fire by sending it through the space resonator. And rejected it because their own Earth Two was badly treated by the original fire. After all, there's no use in staying with a partly ruined, semi-radioactive Earth Two when Earth One, complete and unharmed, lies like a ripe apple for them to pluck."

Maddox nodded. "It will have to be quick," he said. "For either one of them is quite capable of turning the stuff this way once they suspect."

Kingston turned to the kinescope screen and scowled at Virginia and Bronson.

"There," he said, "are two of the four or five people who have within their grasp the truth of the matter—and they are the two who have sufficient imagination to reason it out!"

"And once she kills him that will leave only her!"

Maddox nodded idly and began to set up equipment, saying, "No time like the present."

"For what?"

"I'm interested in knowing whether the atomic fire will burn Earth Three as well as Earth Two."

Kingston shrugged. "Y'know," he said quietly, "if it does ruin Earth Three nothing says that you and I can't pass over ourselves anyway."

Maddox smiled. "Indubitably," he agreed dryly. It was quite obvious that Leader Kingston had given him nothing new in ideas.

Unlike the slow space resonator of Earth Two, the ones used on Earth Three went with lightning swiftness. They were smaller, more efficient, showed a deeper grasp of the art and the principles involved. Maddox picked his collection of equipment up and headed for the door.

"What are you going to use for a focal volume?" demanded Kingston. "You have no focal point."

"Won't need one," smiled Maddox. "That's a true atomic flame. As in the sun there will be minute traces of all elements contained therein and all we need is a trace. For like the sun, Earth Two's atomic flame is both building up and tearing down all elements possible. Come on—I'll prove my point."

For a brief time, Harry Maddox drove like a maniac through the air in his atom-powered speedster. Leaving behind it the whistling scream of its supersonic passage from Albuquerque to Alamogordo, the fleet craft made the passage in minutes. At the site of the original, Maddox landed.

There on the desert was the steel tower that had held the Alamogordo Bomb before its trial. On Earth One there was but a shallow depression of broken green—glazed sand. On Earth Two there burned a pillar of atomic fire for miles in radius from this very spot. Here Maddox set up his space resonator.

Then, sensibly, he urged Kingston back into the speedster and raced away, ten, fifteen miles. Then in his speedster Maddox pressed a button.

Behind them on the desert a burst of intolerable light, like a million suns compressed into a minute sphere, cast its instantaneous glare across the face of the earth. Like an expanding hemisphere of pure sun-flame, it dinned against the very substance of space and hurled its terrible energy outward.

Thunder came then and the still-intolerably bright explosion flashed in multicolored bursts as the shock wave started to rise. Up and up and up into the stratosphere rose the towering ice-cap to roll into a cauliflower shape.

And then up through this bursting-white cloud there darted another pillar of sheer flame-energy, to rise above the first and to go on up into the very upper reaches of the atmosphere.

Standing aghast, Kingston and Maddox watched the scene with horror. Minutes passed before they could speak, and then it was with bitter fear.

Maddox pointed to the ground below the towering pillar of cooling hell. There was a sunlike flame there, burning more brightly by the second. The ground rumbled faintly and, upon the ground at their feet, two shadows were cast which added to the complete unearthliness of the scene.

"Now?" demanded Kingston.

"Not now," growled Maddox angrily. "Our equipment was utterly destroyed in that blast."

"Then we lost?"

"No. All we need do is to return and prepare a radio-controlled speedster to carry another space resonator into the near-scene. Then we can send that pillar of hell back where it came from."

"Think you'll have any trouble?" worried Kingston.

"Nope," said Maddox. "I've been thinking about this for some time. We can do it!"

"Then how are we going to transfer a good bit of that flame to Earth One?"

"I won't mind going over," said Maddox. "I'll see to it that Earth One gets a goodly dose. In fact, I think it might be a good idea to set up a relay system to bring bits of it through and send to other parts of the earth at one time. We can set atomic fires all over Earth One within a matter of seconds."

"Might restart several on Earth Two also," suggested Kingston. "Nothing like speeding things up a bit."

Maddox nodded, but there was a worried frown on his face. "There's one thing I don't relish," he said. "So far as we know, the only bit of radioisotopic phosphor containing the resonant element lies in the laboratory of Ed Bronson on Earth One."

"That's your only doorway?"

"To Earth One, yes."

"Then—"

"Then we return to our vantage point and watch. Sooner or later they will leave that set-up unguarded and we can get through to place other focal elements at a safer place on Earth One."

"Well," smiled Kingston, "once Virginia Carlson gets rid of Ed Bronson they must sooner or later leave that place unguarded and we can break in. Let's go and wait."

"And also prepare the drone to return that pillar of hell back to Earth Two," said Maddox with a bit of mild concern.

Chapter VIII
Halfway Mark

Unmindful of his danger—both immediate and future—Ed Bronson sat and watched Virginia with admiration. Their initial talk had been sketchy. All Virginia knew was that she had been working on equipment similar to his and had heard the same things he had—including him.

Her information was less complete than his, for Virginia was not equipped to tinker up a complete set of filters to tune out the interferences, so she said. Only Bronson's voice came through clearly enough to be understood. Yet she was aware of the danger and felt that she must help.

And that was that so far as she was concerned. As to what track to follow, Virginia professed ignorance. She suggested that they eat and then go to Bronson's laboratory and work on the stuff.

"And what do we do about them?" he asked.

Virginia blinked. "You're certain it was they?"

"He told me so."

"Then there's just one."

"There may be more," objected Bronson. "Perhaps we should forget my place and go to work on yours."

Virginia blinked inwardly at that one. Naturally, Virginia could not take him to her place for she had none. There had to be some way.

"I suggest that you and I go in very quietly," she said. "If the house is infested we'll go to my place. If it is clear, even temporarily, we can go in and steal the phosphor."

"Better," grinned Bronson. "We can conceal it in a steel safe. I have a hunch they can't get through it then."

"I wouldn't know," said Virginia. She did know, however, that Peter Moray would not be in evidence since she was bringing Bronson back with her. "But you have a good idea. It'll do them a lot of good to try coming through if they end up in a steel box.

"Besides," she said thoughtfully, "it is better to try. I'd hate to think of them coming through unguarded. We owe it to the earth to try and stop them."

"That we do," nodded Bronson. Then he ceased to think about it since it had been settled. He preferred to watch Virginia.

She was a beautiful girl—one of the most beautiful women that Bronson had ever seen. That alone won his admiration. But what brought his real commendation was her attitude. Bronson had known other beautiful women before and most of them were inclined towards a selfish narcissism because of the round of admiration they got from every male.

This gave them an egotistical attitude that repelled Bronson, for he knew with some disdain that their attitude was born of the actions of his own sex.

Virginia had none of this false sophistication. She was readily and honestly pleased with things as they were and with Bronson's offerings. To add to that Virginia was clever and intelligent and could, without straining, discuss several subjects that the average beauty wouldn't bother to strain her vapid mind on.

Bronson could not know it, of course, but Virginia's attitude was mostly naiveté. Seldom before had she spent an hour in luxurious surroundings with nothing to think about or to do but relax and enjoy herself. Not that Virginia had forgotten her basic job—but at least here was the offering of relaxation in an atmosphere completely devoid of the constant gnawing fear.

The light in the sky was not there.

Then, too, Virginia was capable of pigeon-holing her mind. Though she intended to eliminate this man as a factor in the safety of her world's people she saw no reason why she should not enjoy herself first. Looking about her in the restaurant she saw many other people enjoying life. This itself was unlike Earth Two and it offered Virginia a point for jealous desire. She wanted this kind of life-without-fear. And it was within her grasp!

In her world many were mutants that repelled the mind. Here there were none. The man opposite her, who toyed with the silverware idly was a fine specimen of humanity. The waiter, the cashier, the hat-check girl, the major-domo, the customers—all were whole and healthy.

Virginia looked about her at the thickly peopled restaurant and mentally compared it with a place in her own world. Idly she replaced the elderly gentleman at the table opposite with a gnarled, seven fingered monster— and the boy-girl couple beyond with a pair of uglinesses.

The waiter instead of being well-dressed and polite was misshapen and clad in remnants of a once-great civilization. Starch wasted on a shirt, as well as the time wasted in preparing it, was unthought-of in Earth Two. Few of the men in Earth Two would look so polished and at ease in the formal trappings.

Bronson made motions to leave and Virginia arose to follow. From his pocket he took money instead of a ration card and he left a generous tip for the waiter. A smiling doorman opened the portal for them.

Once on the street Virginia was again impressed by the people. Then there were the theatre on the corner, the stores and the shops selling anything and everything that men and women would buy.

The automatic bumped Virginia's hip as her bag swung, and the contact hurt—more than physically.

Walking beside this tall man Virginia considered the situation. In her bag was the means of replacing the people she saw in this street with a high percentage of misshapen bodies of her own world. To—eliminate this scene of physical health and mental good-will with the warped bodies and minds of her own world.

Virginia saw her own reflection in a shop window. She was shapely and well-dressed. She knew that without egotism—it was obvious fact. She was more like this world—fitted better into this scene than into the world on which she had been born.

An age-old urge rose in her. She had shied away from marriage because of fear and distaste. Too many of her friends she had seen in mental agony because of mutant offspring. Now she was presented with at least an opportunity of a life that would be normal. What had she on Earth Two but unpleasant memories for all of her life?

Perhaps it seems a sudden change. Yet a mind suddenly shown a way toward happiness will often swing as swift as a pendulum from one attitude to the opposite. Perhaps the only reason that Virginia had not followed many of Earth Two's people into the madness of fear was because she had been born to the insoluble threat of the Alamogordo Blow-up and had never been forced to change from freedom to fear.

Many another on Earth Two had seen the eternal flame and had gone mad, knowing its threat. Virginia, born after it started, had never known anything else. So now Virginia viewed a world built like her own, but one devoid of fear and populated heavily with healthy, happy people.

Why go back? Why change this? She could blend very well with this environment. Her woman's instinct told her that she could and by very little trying.

There was but one great fear. This man who walked beside her knew the facts of Earth Two. He also stood to learn about her. It presented her with a quandary. To make her future secure he must be placed in a position never to learn the truth. On the other hand she needed his aid to forestall the invasion from Earth Two if she were to enjoy the future of Earth One as she now saw it.

Virginia wondered whether she could work with Ed Bronson long enough to give him the particulars of the space-resonant techniques—and still keep him in the dark regarding her own part in it. Once the threat of invasion was gone there was no doubt in Virginia's mind that she could lose herself here on Earth One.

In fact, the proper thing to do was just that—tell him the truth and she would be forever suspect.

Then there was the other problem. She was supposed to have an apartment, a house or something equipped with a basement in which to work. He'd be wanting to see that sooner or later. How to forestall him on that required thinking.

Once he knew that it required the presence of the proper elements in the space-resonant series to effect the transfer of material, he would demand the opportunity of sealing up her bit of the stuff in order to forestall the invasion of the vanguard from Earth Two.

From a technical standpoint, Virginia knew that the operation of the space-resonant science required the presence of the space-resonant elements. Even though she knew nothing of Earth Three and its highly advanced techniques which permitted the operation of a view-and-voice-operated mechanism without the presence of the elements in the area of transmission, Virginia was correct in her assumption that no passage from one time-zone to the other was possible without a critical mass of the ultra-rare transuranic elements in the receptor-zone.

Having used the technique for many years Virginia and the rest in Earth Two could be certain that the only critical mass of these rare elements on Earth One was in Ed Bronson's laboratory.

So, the first thing was to protect herself, to isolate herself on Earth One and to seal up forever the passageway. All Virginia had to do was to break up Ed Bronson's mass into subcritical sizes—and then to keep all other discrete bits of the space-resonant elements from being collected for a period that surpassed the possible time required for the final death of the ill-fated temporal division—the end of Earth Two.

Impulsively, Virginia opened her bag and handed the automatic to Bronson.

"Here," she whispered, "this may help—if they're still here!"

It was hours later. Bronson's re-entry into his home was careful and stealthy but unproductive, for Peter Moray had gone back to Earth Two to await developments. Virginia knew this and was prepared for the lack of population in the Bronson home. Once the place was known to be free of invaders Bronson relaxed.

"Me," he said with a yawn, "I'm tired."

"I don't suppose you got much sleep last night," smiled Virginia.

"Darned little," he agreed. "And I'll get less until we figure out something to do with this equipment of mine. Obviously it does not require energization to permit the effect."

"Why not seal the thing in a metal case of some sort?" suggested Virginia.

"Think it might work?"

"Maybe. At best, if you shield it well and keep it canned up, you can be certain that anybody that comes through will emerge in a dark, confined place."

"Not necessarily," said Bronson. "Radio waves often disregard things like shields and closed rooms. And, if I recall correctly, that feller who came through and clipped me was parked out on the middle of the floor some ten feet from the crystal."

"If you're tired," suggested Virginia, "why not take it easy? You take a snooze and I'll keep watch. You'll think better once you've had a bit of rest."

"But what will you do if—"

Virginia smiled. She went to Bronson and touched his hip pocket with the back of her hand. Ed nodded and took the automatic out of the hip pocket and handed it to her.

"I can't cover eight shots with the ace of spades," she said, hefting the gun, "but I'd not miss an invader."

"I'd like to clip a few of them myself," grunted Bronson. "First I'm up all night. Then I'm clipped by one of them after only a short few hours sleep; then the trip to the asylum, and now home. Yes, Virginia, I've had all too little sleep. You'll be all right?"

"Definitely," she told him. "From here on in, I'm unafraid—and in high confidence."

"Wake me in three hours," he told her. She nodded.

He left, heading toward the bedroom. Virginia found a book and read it quietly, keeping a weather eye on the space-resonant crystal in the experimental kinescope set-up. A half hour later, Virginia put down her book and tiptoed into Bronson's bedroom. He was sprawled on his back in the deepest of slumber.

Virginia went back to his laboratory and began to work on his gear. It was late afternoon when she finished, which was quick enough considering what Virginia had accomplished. It was her field of science, this space-resonant technique, and Ed Bronson's laboratory was rather complete.

So simple, Virginia's plan. Setting a timer to reverse the equipment after a pre-calculated time, Virginia composed herself on a chair and waited. Again, her body faded bit by bit as she passed, molecule by molecule, from Ed Bronson's laboratory. At a short interval beyond the halfway point where Virginia's body sank into the floor, the machine ceased its operation.

Wraithlike, half of her in each world, Virginia was physically powerless. But she knew that her equipment was working. The window of Ed Bronson's laboratory had a strange appearance.

It was not quite like the mixed-image impression received when viewing different scenes simultaneously with the separate eyes. It was more like viewing through a stereoscope, with one side taken in bright sunlight and highly illuminated while the other photo had been taken by moonlight. Also there had been years between the taking of the two because things were not exactly the same.

Of course, Virginia was not viewing one scene with each eye. The process of transmission was not a passage similar to walking through the door. The molecular transfer took place at random, a molecule from here, a molecule from there.

So Virginia viewed the scene in a truly indescribable state. Each eye saw the same scenes—a mixed, foggy montage in poor register.

But the illumination in the afternoon sky was unmistakable as Virginia looked at the window that existed simultaneously in two worlds. She smiled to herself as the equipment in Ed Bronson's laboratory reversed automatically and started to return her to Earth One.

Virginia had been halfway home. And her plan was halfway complete!

Chapter IX
Ill Wind

In the sky, high, high up—a stubby-winged drone circled above Albuquerque thrice. Then it streaked away from the city and headed toward Alamogordo. The pillar of fire was vicious and intolerably bright and it silhouetted the fleet drone—though no one could stand to watch the scene, regardless of the thickness of his eye-glasses.

To all intents and purposes the drone vanished.

But on the viewscreen in Harry Maddox's laboratory the pillar of fire grew, expanded into the entire screen, covered it and made steering ambiguous until Maddox dropped the nose of the fleet little craft so that the field of view included the base of the atomic flame.

The drone arrowed on and on and then came to a machine-made landing a few thousand feet from the base of the flame. Maddox worked swiftly now, for the heat of that devilish fire would ruin the equipment in all too short a time. The equipment went to work.

Then, like the snuffing of a candle flame, the scene went dark. The pillar of fire disappeared and there was a thunderous roar as miles of tortured air raced in to fill the vacuum created by the sudden absence of intolerable heat.

The thunderings shook the city of Albuquerque and the buildings rattled.

In one of the homes Ed Bronson was shaken into wakefulness. He was lying on the floor which was hard though not cold.

He awoke dully. He felt the floor and had a quick impression of having fallen from bed. Grinning sheepishly, Ed Bronson stood up and turned. There was no bed!

The thunderings diminished slowly and Bronson shook his head in wonder. It had not been thunderstorm weather earlier this afternoon. But there was no bed!

"Virginia!" he called, running from the room.

His house was empty of people. In fact his house was refurnished completely. That fact he accepted dully, wondering what had happened and why. It was too great a concept for him to grasp at once. He stared dully at the strange rugs, chairs, appointments. He went into his laboratory—

And found a complete nursery. In one corner was a crib but the infant was missing. It had been used recently, for the bedding was warm—and a bit damp.

Bronson's mind whirled. Strange—strange. But not too strange, considering. If *they* were capable of sending some of their cohorts through the veil that separated the two worlds, it was equally possible for them to reach forth and grab someone from the other world.

Bronson cursed angrily.

He left the house quickly because he knew that, regardless of how he had come here, he was an interloper. Bronson assumed that any of the enemy who might be reaching for him—probably to prevent his forestalling of their efforts—would not merely slip him through the barrier and let him run loose.

Whether something had gone awry in their transmission plans he did not know, but he guessed that something had interfered because no man attempting to grab an enemy would do other than to grab quickly and keep him under supervision.

So Bronson left the house quickly.

He was an interloper—and, though helpless to do anything but run, he was infinitely better off with his freedom than in capture, jail or, more probably, death.

Killing him on his own world would bring about the rather complex problem of disposing of the corpse. While this is possible, it is difficult to dispose of such a high degree of absolute contraband in a civilization with which you are not over-familiar. So some lucky accident had brought Bronson into this ill-fated Earth Two in a residence instead of the laboratory or military establishments of the imminent invaders.

Outside, Bronson knew that something was wrong. He wondered what it was. It was vague, something that was missing from a mere sketchy description but something rather important from a secondary—or was it primary—viewpoint, something that did not jell.

It was late afternoon. The sun was setting in the west. But there was no pillar of atomic fire in the sky!

The Miss Carlson of Earth Two had said that all of Albuquerque was illuminated by the vastness of the pillar of incandescent flame that reached from horizon to the sky. Where in the name of thunder—

The whirling madness spiraled in Bronson's mind with the never-ending round of who, what, why, when and where. And driving that engine of madness was the ever-present and ever-growing fear that the earth he knew was threatened with death—while he could do nothing but stand by and watch it die.

And join it....

The light disappeared like the snuffing of a candle, and Maddox turned to Kingston with a grim smile. "That's that," he said.

Kingston nodded affably. "Now all we have to do is to complete our plans."

Maddox shook his head. "Remember that the stuff in Bronson's laboratory is the only supercritical mass on Earth One. We can see through, of course, but without that focal point we cannot cross over." He turned and left the drone-control room, walking down the corridor towards the other laboratory with Kingston beside him. Kingston was silent for a moment.

Then he nodded in self-satisfaction. "I'll send through a corps of guards to protect it until we need it."

"Better yet," said Maddox, "send through a couple of technicians to separate it into subcritical masses until we need it. Then we can prevent Earth Two from crossing."

They turned the corner of the hallway and entered the original laboratory. As they did so, Kingston caught the sight of the viewscreen and stopped short, his jaw dropping. On the screen was the view of Bronson's laboratory. Virginia was sitting idly in a chair watching the equipment.

Her attitude was not one of complete relaxation, nor was it one of deep intent. Maddox and Kingston knew at once that Virginia was waiting while the equipment ran automatically.

Maddox leaped to the controls of his viewer and followed the cone of energy from the crystal to Ed Bronson's bedroom. There he saw the reason for the work. Ed Bronson's wraithlike body was in the last stages of its disappearance from Earth One.

"So," snapped Maddox. "That takes care of him!"

"Rather clever, too," said Kingston, admiringly. "That's getting rid of a body without fuss or bother or corpus delicti arising somewhere to confront—My Lord! What's she doing?"

Virginia, having seen the equipment come to its end of operation, had run into the bedroom to check on whether Bronson had been transmitted. Maddox had followed her back to Bronson's laboratory and Virginia was opening the tube. She removed the crystalline mass and carried it to the toolbench. Here she placed it on a two-foot slab of mild steel used as a surface plate and was reaching for a hammer with her right hand while her left hand groped for the cold chisel.

Kingston's question was hypothetical. Both men knew what Virginia was about to do.

"Quick!" snapped Kingston. "Stop her!"

"Check!" grunted Maddox, his hands leaping across the control panel.

From the crystal between chisel and surface plate came the beam of invisible energy that enfolded Virginia in its grasp. Unlike the slow process of her own machines, the highly efficient techniques of Earth Three effected the transfer in a matter of milliseconds.

Virginia felt the wrench of a twisted spatial continuum, felt the change as her body adjusted in level and knew briefly that somehow something had gone terribly wrong. The scene before her eyes changed like a flash-over in a moving picture and she faced Maddox and Kingston.

"No you don't," said Kingston roughly.

It was quite wrong. Her trained mind told her that in an instant. Her first brief fear had been that someone from her own world had interrupted her machinations and had grabbed her to prevent the completion of her plans. That would have been quite logical.

But the time interval had been too short. That proved to Virginia that it was not of her own world, for had there been any acceleration in the transfer process, she would have been notified. It was—to her logical mind—quite improbable that such an advance could have been made in the space-resonant techniques in the course of the few short hours during which she had been absent from her own laboratory.

Therefore, she reasoned, there was more to this than met the eye.

She recoiled before the men. Maddox smiled sourly at her and Kingston gloated. "Going to reduce that crystal so that no one could follow you," said Kingston.

"Where—"

Kingston smiled with self-gratification. He felt grandiose enough to gloat a bit more. "This," he said expansively, "is what we term Earth Three."

"Three?" she echoed hollowly.

"Some very brilliant people," chuckled Kingston, "reasoned that there was the possibility of two outcomes to Alamogordo. But they never even considered the possibility of the bomb failing completely. This is the world where the bomb failed."

"Failed!" said Virginia, completely overwhelmed with the implications. Her tone was hollow, almost a psychopathic parroting of Kingston's words. "Failed but...." she was incoherent.

Kingston smiled again. "After all," he said, "the Alamogordo Test was made to determine whether or not the bomb would actually work. Even the finest brains of the day were not certain—and there was the possibility of failure."

"But—"

"Here we are," said Kingston simply.

"But if there was failure?" said Virginia falteringly, but with gaining confidence, "how is it that you are so very well advanced?"

"The failure of the bomb was temporary. A later model worked. But in our world science is completely free and untrammeled. Unlike your world, Virginia Carlson, where science is deeply regulated and directed at one and only one idea, our science knows neither bonds nor interference.

"If you ever get outside in our world you will see atomic power in its fullest use. You will see advances made that are and will always be impossible in any system where a man or a group of men can direct in any way the course of science."

Virginia nodded glumly. "I know," she said. "I've always known of the openings into fields of science that might lead to great things but they were closed because of the necessity of pursuing the one idea toward our future."

Kingston nodded. He admitted the unhappy fact but his own position was none too certain—or had not been until recently.

"If your world is so excellent," asked Virginia bitterly, "why...?"

"The time is approaching when only one future can remain," said Kingston. "No one but an utter egomaniac would consider that the entire universe is regulated for the benefit of mankind. We have yet to make a real attempt to reach the other planets. Have you ever considered the rather impossible proportions of this temporal fission? I doubt it.

"Is, for instance, there a complete universe for each of the time-trails? Or if Earth One and Earth Three both sent rockets to Venus would they meet because Venus was common to both time streams? Think of the energy required to separate a complete universe and ask yourself whether you think it possible."

"Energy has little to do with it," replied Virginia. "Who knows the functioning of the thing we call time—possibly for the want of a better word. Who knows why we have trepidation? Certainly the energy required to cause a planet to falter in its orbit is not truly expended but trepidation is caused by something that seems to require little or no energy."

"We're far from the original premise," said Kingston. "We may never know whether or not the temporal paths are merely local or widespread. It is not a matter of organic versus inorganic matter, for neither is controlled nor directed from any of the other streams of time.

"Were this not so, every time a workman lays a brick on Earth One the same brick would move and be cemented in situ on the other two worlds. And a car on the street might have an accident with a car common to all three worlds but driven only by a driver on Earth One.

"The point is," continued Kingston, "that the time is coming when this triple existence must cease. Again it is the old principle of the survival of the fittest. I am not a firm believer in a god, either benevolent or vicious. Yet there is—or was—some agency that effected this split because it was uncertain as to outcome."

"What hope could there have been for Earth Two?" complained Virginia bitterly.

"Who knows?" replied Kingston. "There might have emerged from her bitter necessity a solution of a lot of ills. Certainly I know that, with the entire world working against that fatal menace, few differences of ideology remain. In Earth Two, Virginia, the lion and the lamb have lain together.

"In fact," grinned Kingston, "you might be closer to allegory to state that the eagle and the bear have a lot in common with lions, dragons and others. It is," he admitted rather unhappily, "a factor that we, here, have not been able to accomplish."

"An ill wind—" said Virginia bitterly.

"True," nodded Kingston. "But the fact remains that the three time paths diverged because of some uncertainty. These same time paths must ultimately come to one ending. We do not know the future—no one does— but this we do know—That world which has the best factor of survival will emerge as the one and only Earth.

"We," said Kingston proudly, "have the best technical perfection, so in any strife we must win. Therefore we are the ones to survive and we are working toward that end. That is why we grabbed you. Your world is doomed. We must ensure the doom of Earth One so that Earth Three is the only one left."

Kingston turned to Maddox. "I think we might be wise to collect Ed Bronson too," he said. "No use letting him run free. Find him and bring him through too."

Maddox nodded and went to work on the controls, setting the dial that determined the depth of penetration to Earth Two. He worked rapidly, sweeping the house that was cojacent with the house on Earth One.

"Heck!" snapped Kingston. "He can't have gone very far. Of course she sent him to her chums. Find them!"

Maddox nodded and located Virginia's laboratory with ease. Moray and Cauldron were there, working on the gear, but obviously getting nowhere. Kingston shrugged. "Cover every place they might conceal Bronson," he directed.

To Virginia, he added, "It is most convenient that Earth Three lies on the other side of Earth One from Earth Two. Were this not so, the fumbling of your friends to penetrate the barrier between the streams of time might cause them to stumble on us."

"Why can't they get through to One?" asked the girl.

Kingston smiled. "Within the hour," he said, "four keys will unlock four safety deposit boxes in four different banks in Albuquerque. Each box contains one subcritical mass of space-resonant elements. My men are finishing the job you started, but this time the key to invasion lies in my hands!" He turned to Maddox, who was fumbling with the controls. "Find him yet?" he demanded.

"No," grumbled Maddox.

Kingston turned to Virginia. "You want to live," he told her in a very matter-of-fact voice, "and therefore it is to your interest to see that we do not permit Bronson to harm our plans. Where is he?"

"I don't know," said the girl. "I merely sent him through."

"You are a brazen little traitor," snapped Kingston. "I believe you! You merely sent him through, you cared not where."

Maddox spoke up. "That equipment she flanged up isn't the most accurate," he said. "But I've covered the entire neighborhood. You know, the closest mass of focal elements lies across the street, in Earth Two, in the laboratory of Virginia Carlson. Therefore, lacking direction and precision, she'd have sent him through to the focal zone of her own gear."

Virginia gasped. Partially blinded as she had been, half-aware of the duplicity of her surroundings, close in the near-paralytic grip of the transmission equipment, Virginia had retained sufficient cognizance to know most definitely that when she looked through the veil, she had been looking into a room that parallelled Bronson's laboratory in shape, size and window-placement.

It was not similar to her own. In her haste she had paid it little attention. Her only thought had been to dispose of the man. Knowing that there were no other critical masses on Earth One, she had felt that anywhere he went was elsewhere.

The implication was clear enough. She had sent Ed Bronson into Earth Three, a simple mistake due to the fact that Two and Three were situated almost equally distant and on opposite sides of Earth One. Obviously, the crude equipment had selected the nearer critical mass—which had been on Earth Three in a cojacent house and not through to Earth Two and across the street to Virginia's own laboratory.

Bronson, then, was on Earth Three, somewhere.

Chapter X
Counterfeit

Bronson found that the streets of the city were teeming with people which was not what he had expected from his brief talk with Miss Carlson of Earth Two. Bronson was absolutely certain that this was not Earth Two at all, for it seemed unlike a world teetering on the brink of death—even ignoring the main clincher of the pillar of atomic fire mentioned by La Carlson, there was that vast and more-than-obvious difference.

Bronson shook his head in wonder. This was not unlike his own world, yet there were subtle differences—subtle differences observable at first glance, but becoming bold and glaring differences as Bronson became more familiar with the street down which he walked.

A bus went past—and did not leave a wake of evil-smelling pale blue exhaust. A store on the corner advertised cigarette lighters which bore the name *Irhinium*. Bronson knew of most of the cigarette lighter companies by name and none of them bore such a name. He looked more carefully and noted that certain vague references to *Irhinium* indicated that it was a trade name based upon the motive power of the things.

In this strange world to which he had been hurled, did they—by the Great Harry—use atomic power to light their cigarettes?

Bronson's mind, of course, was overwhelmed by the suddenness of events and its natural inability to accept such a vast conglomeration of new concepts at the same time. It merely watched, saw, cataloged. Anything outrageous would be given the same consideration as something quite normal in Bronson's nervous state of complete wonder. His mental state bordered on shock.

Noiselessly the traffic moved, noiselessly and without odor. Dress and appointment were brilliant and entirely new. The overhead wires of Ed Bronson's world were gone, as were the poles that bore them. Nor were there street lights. Streetcars plied their routes with a minimum of thundering racket but there was neither trolley above nor slot in the street below.

Bronson paused before a large toy shop and watched a man manipulating an electric train. The miniature train had all the maneuverability of a real train because of the multiplicity of controls under the fingers of the man in the window. Beside the train was a large box containing cubic bits of metal and non-metal.

The explanation on the box said that the contents would build a miniature fission-reacting pile that worked but which employed Kenium metal instead of uranium since the use of the latter was dangerous, requiring ton upon ton of fissionable material as well as a moderator.

That was the clincher.

Bronson's mind cleared once the facts were driven home. He was not on Earth Two. He was most certainly not on Earth One.

But Ed Bronson's mind leaped to the foregone conclusion with simple reasoning. Earth One, Earth Two—and Earth Three, where the third possibility had taken place at Alamogordo, on July sixteenth, 1945. This was where the bomb had fizzled—and where, because of that, all forms of atomic research went on without regulation.

Not one world, not two worlds, *but three!*

Well, there was a perfect way to check this. Bronson knew where the library was, had used it often. It might still be there, for the one in Earth One had been erected in—ah—he did not recall the date but it was something like MDCCCLXXXVI.

He turned the corner and walked down the proper street and, after turning the second corner, Bronson saw it—in the same address and in the same building. He wasted no time in finding the newspaper files.

July sixteenth, 1945, was uninformative. Bronson wondered what the same paper printed in his own world said on that date but guessed that this paper, a morning daily, might have been composed and on the press at the time of the affair—if it had not been already printed.

Of security angles for the era he studied, Bronson knew only the mention made in history and tales spun by his father and cronies, who had lived and worked at that time. So Bronson accepted the fact that security might well have suppressed in both worlds—or even all three—any traces of the Alamogordo Experiment for some time to come.

He turned to the following day, July seventeen, 1945, and found nothing. On the eighteenth, Bronson saw nothing truly informative but there was an item printed as recorded from Radio Tokyo in which it was claimed that the

United States had asked for representatives of the Japanese Government to come to America under a flag of truce. This was construed to mean that the United States was considering surrender.

Nothing was visible for several issues after that. Then a vast headline—PEACE—shouted across the page and on page two of the paper, was a brief explanation that the representatives had returned to Japan. A columnist was demanding an answer to what and why the mystery.

Another account from Radio Tokyo mentioned that, in a spirit of humanity, Japan had surrendered rather than loose upon the entire world a weapon so terrible as the representatives had been shown.

Bronson nodded vaguely. The trail was getting intelligible. He at least knew nothing of this latter fact. He thumbed his way through the paper to the date of the Hiroshima Bomb and found nothing worthy of mention. Nagasaki was not mentioned a week or so later and Bronson, none too clear of his dates, covered days before and after his approximation just to be certain.

He pored through the paper and found many references to the Manhattan Project, including one full newspaper, on the general lines of what he recalled of the Smyth Report.

A month later a Washington columnist printed a scoop. There had been a test of an atom bomb at Alamogordo, he claimed, and the bomb had failed to function.

"Ah," said Bronson aloud.

What came next? How the two worlds had become so socially and technically different was something to be studied at a later date. For the present Bronson felt that it was the time to start thinking about action.

He left the library and walked down the street thoughtfully. Here the bomb had failed, here—and automatically Ed Bronson cataloged the place as Earth Three—science was unfettered.

So, he reasoned along two lines simultaneously, the transmission of things from one plane to the other required the use of the radioisotopic phosphor—Bronson did not know the conglomeration of transuranic elements comprised an entire rare element group known as the space-resonant series and so called them by the name he had known them—and since this was so, he would be forced to investigate.

Also, since Earth Three had no apparent regulation on scientific research, it would probably be easy to obtain enough to go to work. The unfortunate part of it was that his rather extensive bank account was deposited in the First National Bank. Though it was situated within three blocks of this very spot, its officers would view his very solid checks as so much illegal paper.

He smiled wryly.

So here he was, isolated on an obviously alien world, with the weight of his own earth on his shoulders, quite incapable of more than scratching the surface.

Lost—completely lost—in the troubled thought, Ed Bronson's trained hands, by sheer reflex, dipped into his pocket for a cigarette. The hands, finding none, notified the locomotor areas of his brain, which, operating on sheer habit and reflex, sent a message to the eyes.

The eyes looked around, though what they scanned made no impression on the more conscious sections of Bronson's mind. They caught what was wanted and the automatic process went on—the information went back to the habit-section, directions went to the muscles and Bronson walked towards the drug-store in absolutely the same state of coma as the proverbial absent-minded professor.

Too deeply engrossed in his thoughts to pay attention to the automatic items, Ed Bronson's brain caused his voice to murmur a cigarette-brand name. The cigarette came, and Bronson's right hand dipped into his pocket and dropped a twenty-dollar bill on the counter.

The clerk looked at it and mumbled, "Have to get change, mister."

Again unconsciously, Bronson's head nodded.

Had anything evolved that was out of the normal routine, Bronson would have been forced to take notice. But this was like driving an automobile or riding a bicycle. It required no conscious effort so long as nothing demanded decision.

Nothing demanded decision. The decision was made for him. He felt a heavy hand on his shoulder and felt it turn him so that he faced—His mind came back to his surroundings like a snapped rubber band. A policeman!

"What's the idea?" demanded the latter.

"What idea?" asked Bronson.

"Counterfeit money."

"That isn't it—"

The policeman laughed nastily. "Looks perfect," he admitted. "But I might point out that E. Thomas Froman is not the secretary of the United States Treasury."

"Huh?" grunted Bronson.

"A perfect counterfeit excepting that the wrong fellow signed it," snapped the policeman. "What's the idea, fellow? I take it you don't mind counterfeiting but dislike being jailed for forgery?"

"I don't get it."

"You will," smiled the policeman with great self-satisfaction. "Come along. Counterfeit money is a bad thing to have in your possession."

Bronson cursed himself. He had even more.

Anticipating distastefully his second visit to the police station in as many days, Ed Bronson emerged from the squad car behind the policeman. This was one of the basic differences. This was not by far the same place he had been in before and the seriousness of his position made Ed Bronson smile whimsically.

If not the only one ever to do it, he believed himself at least the first man ever to be jailed in two jails on two worlds—or on one world separated by only time. It was "doing time" with a vengeance!

With the policeman following him, Bronson went into the building, upstairs and into a room filled with scientific equipment. His quick mind decided that, on this world, advances had also been made in criminology. But he was forced to wait and see, for none of the equipment made sense to Bronson. What the police did with it, how it separated criminal from citizen, Bronson had no idea.

"—passed a twenty dollar bill signed by E. Thomas Froman as Secretary of the United States Treasury," said the policeman.

"Clever of you, officer."

"Thank you. The shopkeeper merely assumed it to be counterfeit. I knew better."

"This, officer, is Ed Bronson—of Earth One," said Kingston.

Bronson jumped visibly. They knew him! Then he realized that they must certainly know him because they had kidnaped him through the barrier in time. This, of course, was erroneous, for it had been Virginia's machinations that had brought him here. On the other hand, the error made little difference so far as its end-result went, for it was true that they knew him and also that they were quite glad to have him under their thumbs.

"So you're the birds who grabbed me?" he said brashly.

Kingston grinned wolfishly. He saw little reason for letting Bronson know that another had accomplished what he himself had wanted.

"We're glad to see you," said Kingston.

"No doubt," snapped Bronson. "The pleasure is all yours."

"Don't be petty," laughed Kingston.

Bronson turned around to see what the other man—Maddox, of course—was doing. Maddox had stopped using the space-resonant viewer, but the screen depicted a street on Earth Two, which was obvious since there were twin shadows cast, one by the sun and one by the atomic flame.

Bronson knew it by reputation if in no other way. So he nodded at it and said, scathingly, "Convenient way to spy on your neighbors, isn't it?"

Kingston nodded and smiled. And Bronson knew that the real menace to Earth One was not the fear-filled, already-dying Earth Two with its growing cancer of atomic flame, but this free, lusty Earth Three where science had been unrestricted in scope and field and direction.

Superior in the knowledge that they controlled the entire situation because of their higher degree of varied sciences, men of Earth Three were quite capable of biding their time and aiding in any scheme planned by Earth Two—or perhaps Earth One—that would enhance the future of Earth Three.

Bronson saw them as conquistadores, watching savages fight over a lush island and waiting for the least difficult moment to release all the terrors of modern civilization to defeat both sides.

"So what happens to me?" he snapped.

"Unwittingly you have served us," said Kingston. "We could not get through to you so long as you possessed no critical mass of the space-resonant elements—"

"What—"

"Among the chemical compounds you were playing with, there are several of the transuranic elements created by the atomic pile," explained Kingston, falling back into his superior attitude. "These form a rare-element group known as the space-resonant series and they respond to one another in many ways.

"Some of them are bizarre compared to the theories held by your so-called modern physics. We use them as matter transmitters and it is a rare home that has none for the delivery of merchandise."

"So?"

"So," laughed Kingston, "when you finally collected your critical mass you enabled us to enter your Earth One, as we call it."

"And?"

"Your engineer's mind can reason out the rest," replied Kingston quietly.

"You mean that sooner or later one of the three must cease?"

"Yes. To prove it, I shall pose a question. Have you ever considered whether the entire universe was following triple time-paths or whether it is only this section of the universe?"

"Not vitally," replied Bronson.

"Then think about it," said Kingston. "You'll have time."

"I—?"

"You'll have time. We have the power and the science and the will and the ability to effect those necessary factors that will cause Earth Three alone to survive."

Bronson was forced to admit that Kingston was quite correct. Though he said nothing nor gave any sign that he agreed, Bronson was forced to agree that Earth Three was deep in its plans while Earth One lay complacently in ignorance of its danger. The only man who had any inkling of their danger was himself—and he had tried to warn them only to be greeted as a lunatic.

He wanted desperately to know about Virginia but was afraid to ask— or even to show that he had hope. If she were back there and safe—

Kingston smiled tolerantly. "You might as well relax," he said. "There will be no return to Earth One for anybody until we are ready." He explained about the division of the space resonant elements into four subcritical masses. "It even prevents those from the doomed Earth Two from entering."

Bronson remained silent.

"And the stuff in your laboratory is the only critical mass existent on Earth One," added Kingston.

Bronson's heart leaped and it was with all of his effort that he kept that gleam of hope from showing. They did not know nor had they detected the mass used by Virginia in her laboratory—could it be because her set-up was inefficient as she admitted? Bronson breathed a prayer that they would never find out.

But it gave him hope—a hope that permitted him to relax for the moment instead of breaking into action, however futile. Bronson's feelings had been one of frustration, an almost overwhelming desire to beat his fists against something even though it was futile—the insane desire to strike a blow, however minute.

"Until later," said Kingston, "you will occupy a room upstairs. Whether or not you survive with us will depend upon how you behave. I assure you that dying for a principle is futility personified and that a live traitor surpasses a dead fanatic."

Chapter XI
Reunion on Earth Three

In a small but comfortable room in Maddox's laboratory Bronson found time to object to Kingston's statement that anyone adhering to a principle is automatically a fanatic. A fanatic, according to one of Bronson's rather cynical definitions, was any man who adhered to a set of principles at variance with your own.

Time went on slowly and it became dark eventually. Bronson could hardly believe that he had been a free and happy scientist but a few days ago, that all that had happened to him had occurred in so short a time.

He had taken a few hours of sleep not long ago but it was insufficient. Now, with the entire program at a standstill, nervous reaction set in and the enforced inactivity drove Bronson deep into the fatigue he had been ignoring because of nervous energy. He sprawled on the bed and stared at the ceiling for a short time—and then slept.

Bronson awoke much later and saw by his watch that it was about three o'clock in the morning. By then he was slept out and quite ready to test his brain and his body against Kingston and Maddox.

Lying on the bed Bronson tried to plan.

The main problem was to effect an exit and take a look around—cooped up here he could do nothing at all. His mind, having been geared to fast action for days, was now craving more action. It was like a drug. And a portion of his mind told him that if all this could happen in a short time, there was reason to believe that more concentrated action might solve the puzzle.

So Bronson arose and inspected the door. The place had not been designed as a prison. The door was a normal door and the lock was a flimsy affair intended to serve merely as a warning to the uninvited that the room was forbidden. It would give no trouble at all to someone determined to enter—or to get out.

Bronson smiled in the dim moonlight. Undoubtedly, Kingston felt that, with no place to go, Bronson's freedom was unimportant.

He went to the closet and found a couple of wire coat-hangers. One of these he twisted into a small hook to probe the lock. It was a simple single-tumbler bolt lock and Bronson lifted the tumbler easily and slid the bolt back. The door opened on oiled hinges and he was in the clear.

His first move was to the street door. That was heavily locked and barred and, engineer that Ed Bronson was, picking a lock of that calibre was beyond his ability. He checked the windows but every window was equipped with a slender, ornamental grille-work that was as effective a barrier as the plain bars of the average jail.

Bronson shrugged. Whatever the score, whatever the outcome, he had to make some move. Not the kind of idiotic physical strife against Kingston and his minions which would get him only a broken head with nothing gained, but some move based upon the thing that Bronson knew best. He knew little of the space-resonant communicator but there was a bare chance of his finding out.

Virginia—what had happened to her in the melee? Had she escaped and, if so, could he communicate with her from Kingston's gear upstairs. Or was Virginia also a prisoner in this scientific mausoleum?

Questions all—and no answers. Bronson felt complete futility once more.

He raced upstairs. If the space resonator would cross the temporal rift to Earth One, it would also cross to Earth Two. Perhaps, he reasoned, with greater difficulty because Earth One was the focal point and the more stable. And, if what little he knew about Earth Two were correct, Earth Two might well never learn of Earth Three despite the presence on all hands of the focal elements.

Delving into the lesser facets of a science was not permitted on Earth Two. Some high brass on Earth Two must have viewed the transmission possibilities of the space-resonant elements and decided that they were to be used for transportation and communication and nothing more. Some brass with fear, pardonably ignorant of the fact that just beyond his fingertips in the depths of an unknown science lay hidden the secret that would give them hope.

So much for regulated science!

The equipment was mostly of mass-manufacture. That helped. Nameplates were written in plain enough English and the controls were not difficult to understand. Bronson studied it quite some time before making his first move, then reached forward and snapped on the master switch.

He turned the switch marked "video" and the screen came to life. Maddox had made pencil-marks on the power dial to indicate the depth of penetration necessary to reach both of the other temporal worlds. Bronson tried Earth One gingerly and saw his own home. Maddox had left the controls set when the news of Bronson's capture had come.

Bronson tried the steering controls and sent the plane of view along the silent street of his own world. It went on a skew because the line-up of angles was imperfect and Bronson found that he had to manipulate a side-swing control in conjunction with the line control to keep the plane of view from angling off into the houses that lined the street.

Then, with the equipment's secrets available for him to study, Bronson abandoned such study in order to think and plan more thoroughly.

The lock upon his door was certainly not the kind that any man in his right sense would use to imprison any but a schoolchild. That did not ring true, even though Kingston and Maddox held him in contempt and knew that Bronson could never return to Earth One.

There was more to it than that. He turned back to the equipment and set the depth-dial to zero-zero. Then, with an amused shock, Bronson was looking at a view of himself who was looking at the viewscreen upon which was the same picture. Lack of definition in the picture elements prevented the scene from being repeated to the infinitely small.

But there was no time for fooling. So Ed Bronson lifted the plane of view and passed the plane entirely through the top floor of the building. He brought it back once it had reached the back and repassed it again, setting it aside by nine-tenths of its span. On the fourth pass Bronson saw something, plucked at the switches and rotated the plane of view.

Here was a small room. Two cots were there with a sleeping man in each. They were in uniform. A third man lounged in an easy chair—asleep.

Bronson breathed more easily. For, on a small portable viewer, was the bedroom that Bronson had recently vacated. Guards, obviously, and one of them luckily eligible for court-martial for sleeping on his watch!

Bronson spun the distance dial wildly, and saw a kaleidoscope of color, land, rock, and stream. He cared not where it was that he came upon the supercritical mass of space resonant elements—all he cared was that it was a goodly distance away.

He did smile when he saw the name of the store on the window—not that he could read it for, to Ed Bronson, lettering in Russian might as well be read from either inside or outside or upside-down or backwards—because he had a hunch that uniformed guards trying to explain their undesirable presence in a Russian store would be at a loss to explain how they had got there.

His hand found the key marked TRANSMISSION and he saw all three guards land on the hard cold floor, awake, and start to ask themselves what had happened.

He left them to their wonder, though he admitted that at any less strenuous time it would be most interesting to watch their complete discomfort and amazement. He brought back the scene of view and continued to pass the plane back and forth through the building. On the floor below the guards—in the apartment next to his own place of imprisonment—the field of view passed over a bed. A tousle of hair and an outstretched arm caused Bronson to blink.

"Virginia!" he breathed.

They had captured her, too. Well. That meant some saving in time. Virginia would help him. Since the mass of crystals in his own lab had been reduced to non-operative masses and well separated, the only other possible mass was that in Virginia's place. What they would do, of course, was to get back on Earth One and subdivide her crystals into ineffectual masses and then instigate a search for the parts of his own. Once he locked the invaders out they could so remain forever.

Bronson nodded happily. He continued to sweep the plane of view through the building until he came upon Maddox and Kingston. With a grin, he delivered both of them to the same store in Siberia and then returned to the contemplation of his problem.

It seemed a shame to abandon all this gear. And if he took Virginia back with him, through this machine, someone would know instantly where they had gone. There was no known way of fouling up the controls after no one was left in the laboratory to do it.

And despite his amusement at the idea of several irate people trying to explain to an irate officialdom why, how and wherefor, Bronson knew very well that Kingston and Maddox would be able to talk their way home in all too short a time.

Certainly far too short a time to transport the equipment he wanted.

Virginia? Bronson shrugged. He kept forgetting that she knew actually less about this sort of thing than he did. She had said that her gear was far less efficient than his.

Bronson sent the plane of view skimming forward across the earth again, and then thoughtfully set it for Earth Two. Far away from New Mexico, in the lake region of Northern Michigan, Ed Bronson found a small cottage—untenanted but with a supercritical mass of the space-resonant elements available.

Then Bronson expanded the volume of transmission to its utmost, turned up the variac on the line voltage to overload proportions to add to the general increase and then, wondering if he were rushing in where an angel would fear to tread and also remembering that a little knowledge is often a very dangerous thing, Ed Bronson shoved the transmitting switch in with a gesture of finality....

Upstairs, in the room next to Bronson's previous place of imprisonment, Virginia Carlson, formerly of Earth Two, was sleeping easily. Her first big decision had been made—her decision to accept the pleasant aspect of Earth One forever, eschewing her former life. People who insist upon absolute loyalty will scorn her decision. Yet from a pragmatic standpoint, Virginia was correct even though she may have been morally and ethically wrong.

For her own Earth Two had been a sorry place indeed, peopled with neurotics and hopeless mutants, the population more than decimated by the bomb and its radiation effects. Of a minor percentage of the population of Earth Two, Virginia was inclined to view the wholesome and happy population of Earth One as her own kind. Certainly, as a whole and healthy woman in all senses of the word, Virginia did belong.

The decision had not been made without a wrench. It had most definitely been a huge decision. It is never easy to give up an existence completely even though it is less than desirable because of loyalties and friendships made.

Yet the practical aspect was important. Nature—human nature—had created Virginia's decision, not the girl herself. For her life on Earth Two, threatened as it was with extinction within a few short years, violated the very concepts of nature.

First, there is the eon-old instinct for self-preservation. Few mentalities will accept self-negation for the benefit of other people. No stable mentality will accept self-negation when it means little to anyone.

And why her subconscious mind reasoned, should she aid in the destruction of a healthy civilization for the benefit of a civilization already doomed?

No more selfish than anyone else, Virginia knew that nothing she could do would render the people of her own world a healthy race—not after radiation and death and the nerve-shattering fear had taken its toll for thirty years. So Virginia's initial decision had been made.

Then had come Earth Three. And once the abandonment of the first principle had been done, Virginia no longer had loyalty upon which to fall back. Once the idea of self-preservation had come to the fore, it was a mere matter of selecting her future from the practical standpoint alone.

Earth Three certainly had what it took to win. In a culture unhampered by brass-hattism science had made vast strides. From her history she knew that science was a vital factor in any strife and had been for a century or more.

No longer was it possible for a group of farmers to rebel and make it stick. In the American Revolution any armed man was as good as any armed soldier—better in many cases since the armed farmer was not restrained by certain codes and restrictions.

But for years the armed farmer, though willing and able, was not possessed of the weapons of modern warfare. Tanks are not needed on a farm. Flamethrowers are not a household item. Machine-guns are inefficient against ducks and geese. Pursuit aircraft and bombers do not find much service in a peacetime civilization.

So science had removed the concept of Mr. Colt's Equalizer, for while the Colt made all men equal, its superior developments rendered a trained and equipped army far superior to the most avid of citizen armies.

In a similar vein Earth Three, with its unbounded science was, without a doubt, more capable of survival in this affair.

Especially when their objective, Earth One, was lying silently, enjoying its luxury, and not even suspecting the widespread preparations going on. Earth One would be swarmed under and destroyed before it realized what was going on.

Well, reasoned Virginia, since she had decided to accept a future, eschewing her former life on Earth Two, it remained only for her to accept whichever future seemed the most secure.

So Virginia Carlson slept easily, feeling that she had, by chance or by luck, been inserted into the one future that promised the most. Her dreams were untroubled.

The building groaned in the cry of tortured metal and stone. It dropped in a plaster-cracking jar a full half yard, then tilted swiftly to one corner and stopped, settling gradually as the slack was taken up. The roaring groan ceased and left only the crackling sound of fissures running through concrete, the flaking of scale from ironwork, and unimportant splintering and cracking of timber.

Virginia awoke with a cry of fear.

She heard footsteps on the stairs and she wondered what had happened. She knew that Maddox and Kingston were experimenting and wondered whether they had touched off something dangerous. Earthquake came to mind and she wondered about it.

Earthquakes were nothing new to Virginia, since the atomic fire that burned deep into the bowels of Earth Two had released surface strain from time to time as it ate its way through compressed rock-strata.

She sat up in bed and reached for her clothing. No matter what it was it was still better to face trouble dressed.

She was slipping into her frock when the door burst open and, there was Ed Bronson—whom she believed that she had sent to Earth Two. Virginia recoiled automatically.

**There was Ed Bronson—whom she
believed she had sent to Earth Two.**

"Hi," said Bronson cheerfully.

Virginia blinked—mentally, actually and figuratively. According to her mental record of the proceedings, Bronson had every right to extract any penalty he deemed fit.

Dubiously, she replied, "Hi."

"Cheer up," he told her, not noticing her nervousness. "I've just swiped the entire batch—the whole shooting match. Now we can work this out all by ourselves."

Virginia nodded vaguely.

Bronson noticed her uncertainty. "I've just expanded the field of focus or whatever it's called that used to transmit stuff from one temporal plane to the other—and I've shoved you, me, building, foot, horse and marines into Earth Two to get away from that gang."

Virginia recoiled mentally. After all the mad work, the planning, the acceptance of a plan intended to place her in a more desirable future, here she was right back in Earth Two—doomed once more to the creeping atomic flame.

Chapter XII
Dawn in Flame

Virginia followed Bronson down to the laboratory in a daze, and she comprehended only about one half of what he was saying. The one thing that she did not understand was why he knew nothing of Earth Two. She believed she had sent him there and the double transfer should have awakened him.

That should have left him aware of his transfer to Earth Three when Kingston kidnaped him.

Kingston could have told her that the bright sky light she saw in her half-state had been but the temporarily-transferred atomic flame but Kingston was not there. So instead of wanting to kill her summarily for her double-cross, Ed Bronson still believed that she was originally of Earth One, had been kidnaped as he had been.

Virginia did find it a bit amusing—perhaps it was the hysteria that acts as a safety valve when things are so unreasonable that the mind will not accept them without seeking its funny side.

Dawn was breaking as Bronson finished his explanation and, as the light increased, he turned to the equipment and said, "We've got this all to ourselves here. I couldn't find your crystal on Earth One—and besides, if Kingston can flange up some means of detecting the presence of the stuff on Earth One, there'd be but that one to detect.

"And I couldn't set this mausoleum down on Earth One near any city street. No room. I'm assuming that your diggings are in the city?"

He did not wait for Virginia to answer, but turned to the equipment and started to look it over in earnest. "This," he said, "I've got to know more about."

Virginia could have told him but she merely nodded vaguely and said nothing. She thought it over.

"Have you any hope at all of saving your world?" she asked—and then gasped because she had not said "our world."

She might have saved her fear, for he did not notice. "Some," he said, straightening up from the gear and looking at her with a half smile.

"Do I sound disloyal," she said tremulously, "if I suggest that if Earth Three wins we have the means here to join them?" Virginia hoped to gain some idea of his feelings on the subject so that she could calculate his intentions.

Bronson shook his head grimly. "Earth Three," he said, "appears to have all the cards. No one doubts that Earth Two is doomed and is no true menace compared to Three. Earth Three is cognizant of its possible fate and is most certainly working furiously to avoid it."

"They plot and plan against Earth One while Earth One sleeps in the peace of false security. Lord knows, I've tried to tell them, and they are so incapable of understanding this affair that they tried to slap me in the clink for believing it." He laughed bitterly. "When I was a kid in school they tried to tell me that any man who tells the truth has nothing to fear."

"But if Earth Three wins—as it seems certain to do?" she insisted.

"That would be bad," he said.

"Why?"

"Virginia," he said soberly, "I don't quite know what it is but there's something very wrong with Earth Three. Confound it, it's simple enough, too, but for the life of me I cannot see it."

"What can be wrong with a world where science and knowledge are not suppressed?"

"I don't know," he said irritably. "But there's something wrong with Earth Three." He turned back to the gear again. "The one thing we must be on the watch for is the day when Kingston sends word for his trustees to assemble his space-resonant materials into a supercritical mass.

"Also we must watch to see that he does not use yours. I'm going to duplicate this equipment first and then your job will be to keep an eye on Kingston all the time while I work out this stuff."

Bronson looked around him with a cynical smile. "Books, data, equipment, and supplies," he said. "This is not like finding the science of an ancient culture. This is a man finding a complete means of study of a science of his own civilization removed but a few years to the future.

"I've often laughed," he went on cheerfully, "at what Volta and Henry might think if they saw a modern circuit. But give them books, equipment and material and they would work it out soon enough.

"Radio, for instance, would have had its inception in the middle of the nineteenth century if twentieth century measuring and testing equipment and books had been handy. So," he strode over to a bookcase and took out a heavy tome, "we work this out."

Virginia shook her head unhappily. "Why, oh why did this thing happen?"

Bronson smiled tolerantly. "Because of the chances," he said thoughtfully. "I'm no believer in a great and benevolent god who interferes with his subjects. I'm more inclined to look upon God as an intellect interested in the problems of his subjects and quite willing to let them work out their own destiny—if for no other reason than to discover whether He had built well.

"You cannot know how good your toy is if you insist upon helping it over the difficult places with your hands. It must run of itself to be a good model.

"Now I'm not exactly convinced that Nature or God was baffled by this thing that His toy built and therefore held His benevolent—but baffled— hand in the stream of time to see which was the best.

"I'm inclined to think there was a good scientific explanation of why time should have split three ways—why in one case the earth entered fission, why the thing worked properly in another time-stream and why the Alamogordo Bomb fizzled in a third."

"Can you find out why—and what it could have been?" she asked.

He laughed shortly. "It isn't mumbo-jumbo or magic," he said. "All of the things attributed to mumbo-jumbo are based upon facts not known to those who observe the effects. The very fact that there was some doubt about the outcome of the Alamogordo Bomb proved that the best brains knew their knowledge of nuclear physics was incomplete."

Virginia nodded brightly. "So you think that some unknown factor caused the trouble?"

"Obviously. We know that fissionable materials do operate. The Hiroshima and Nagasaki bombs were of different types of material, giving us at least two different proofs of its operation. We have too little knowledge of Earth Three but I'm reasonably certain that, once the original experiment failed, fissionable reactions took place and are taking place now. We know even less of the affair of Earth Two. We don't know but can assume that later attempts would turn out properly."

Virginia said nothing. She nodded sagely, and her nod was based upon the fact that she knew he was right but could not say so lest she be forced to tell the rest of her story.

"So," he said, "we can assume that something was either generated or present in the mixture at Alamogordo that, in one case, stopped the reaction, in the next case, permitted the thing to work and, in the third case, started the atomic fire in the earth."

"How do you go about finding it?" she asked. Virginia was interested. This theory was new to her, but it sounded reasonably solid.

He grinned unhappily. "The trouble with making experiments in atomic explosions is that it leaves so little stuff to measure afterwards." He lifted a crystal of the space-resonant elements and looked at it with wrinkled forehead.

"Something in this crystal holds the answer. I think we should analyze this material right down to the most infinitesimal trace. Then we can find out which of the included elements is responsible for the original problem."

"I can help," said Virginia.

He smiled grimly. "Your job is to keep an eye on Maddox and Kingston. See if you can locate their men on Earth One, also see what you can do toward locating those four subcritical masses. We must keep Kingston and the rest of his gang from entering Earth One." He looked at her thoughtfully. "Also keep an eye on your own collection."

Virginia smiled and nodded. She looked him squarely in the eye and said, "My collection of those elements is very small."

"Um," he said. "It's more than possible that the various functions of the space-resonant elements depends upon their mass. For instance, a small quantity might be suitable for mere communication—a larger quantity may be required for the visual communication, while a still larger mass is needed for a physical transfer.

"How their division comes with respect to the transfer of objects or messages from time plane to time plane is something that might be baffling."

"But what are you going to do right now?" asked Virginia.

"First, I'm going to see what can be done about building a detector for the supercritical masses," he said. "Then we're going to do some micro-analysis on these crystals."

Virginia was silent. She was not entirely convinced that there was something wrong with the culture on Earth Three. Earth Three obviously had all of the scientific cards, what with years of research and no restrictions or regulations.

However, Virginia was content to remain where she was for a short time. There was little point in making an abrupt change just then. Any moment that danger threatened Virginia knew that she could escape to Earth Three and be safe. Her decision to remain was based upon her lifetime of training on Earth Two.

Regardless of any decision to eschew a former life, the training of a lifetime will remain. That Virginia had no intention of remaining on Earth Two did not remove her interest in the main problem of her life. Bronson had some theories that were interesting. Therefore Virginia was content to remain and learn all she could.

Such knowledge might come in handy at a later date.

Leader Kingston leaned back against a counter and regarded his cohorts with a cold stare. Maddox growled in his throat and the three guards cowered because theirs had been a crime punishable by death for hundreds of years.

"Well," asked Maddox, "what do we do now?"

"The first thing," said Kingston sharply, "is to locate ourselves."

"That shouldn't be hard," said Maddox, looking around. Kingston nodded, regarding his wrist watch.

"It is near-morning in New Mexico," he said. "Where we are now is midnight."

"It's also cold—and that lettering on the window is Russian. We are in eastern Siberia."

Kingston made some calculations. "We're lucky at that," he said. "So long as morning comes in Washington before morning comes here we are in no great danger. The fact is," he added, regarding his watch once more, "that the monitors will be taking up their regular duty in a few minutes. Otherwise we might have no end of trouble."

Maddox shrugged. A pajama-clad man has little dignity and very little authority. To be trapped in a foreign country—one whose politics differ from your own—under highly suspicious circumstances might well result in a long period of enforced inactivity. Bronson had been in a hurry when he had performed the shipping operation. Had he taken time to think it over, Bronson would have sent them to some place where their arrival would have brought them instant apprehension.

But Bronson had been in a hurry and his only desire was to ship them to some spot not fitted with instant means of escape. He would have preferred some place where no space-resonant element existed but that was impossible since the technique demanded a focal mass.

"So," said Kingston, showing Maddox the silvery-metal band on his wrist, "as soon as the monitors take over and locate me, we'll—"

He disappeared in mid-sentence and Maddox followed a few seconds later. The guards vanished at regular intervals, leaving the Russian store vacant once again.

Minutes later Kingston and Maddox emerged from a standard transmission building not far from the site of the laboratory. Maddox was puzzling openly. "Bronson has probably ripped the tuning circuit from my receiver," he said. "But what would that gain him?"

"Only a few minutes more time," said Kingston. "Instead of our landing back home again, we must use a standard line and walk a few squares. I—look!"

"Heaven!" breathed Maddox.

The laboratory site was, naturally, vacant.

"I didn't think it possible," said Maddox.

"But where did he take it?" wondered Kingston.

"Who knows?" said Maddox, spreading his hands.

"We can find out but it will take time. My guess is Earth Two somewhere. He'd be a fool to stay here where he can be found easily."

"It wouldn't be too easy if Bronson has hashed up the keyed tuning circuit," grunted Maddox angrily. "Confound it, that reduces the problem to one of searching two worlds for the right mass of elements."

Kingston shook his head. "We're about ready," he said. "Give us another week or so and we can eliminate all opposition." His face hardened. "In fact, we can start to spread the atomic fire on Earth Two at any time."

They turned back to the standard transmission building and returned to Washington. There was nothing they could do without the laboratory and there were other, well-equipped laboratories in Washington. Actually, so far as the operations in the space-resonant bands were concerned, location meant very little. It had been merely convenient to locate in Maddox's place.

Once returned to Kingston's official building, the leader set his operatives to checking the supercritical masses in the vain hope of locating one of them that existed in the stolen laboratory.

Bronson's statement that he wanted a detector did not mean none existed. All forms of communication require the two main components—generator and detector. Kingston's men, to track down the stolen laboratory, merely tuned through the space-resonant bands, stopping every time they hit a response so that they could check the neighborhood visually.

What Bronson wanted was not a mere detector. He wanted some means of knowing definitely when the subcritical masses of his own space-resonant elements were reassembled. This is comparable to a device that will register whenever a radio transmitter is turned on, regardless of frequency or location.

Bronson knew that the tuning qualities of the space-resonant effects depended mostly on the mass of the crystals. He knew the mass of his own stuff but that had been formed to serve as fluorescent material and the amount of the space-resonant elements in that mass was uncertain—especially in view of the fact that Earth One was still to learn of the space-resonant bands.

So Bronson's knowledge of the mass of his own crystal did not include the proportion of these new elements and therefore he had little knowledge of how the divided masses would resonate.

It was quite a project—but it had to be done.

Chapter XIII
To Find the Plan

Cautiously, Virginia entered the laboratory and peered over Ed Bronson's shoulder. "What are those?" she asked.

"Amplifiers," he explained. "I'm hoping to locate the subcritical masses."

Virginia looked dubious. "Where did you get them?" she asked.

He grinned boyishly, "Stole 'em. I searched the laboratories of Earth Three and came up with four of their best. Earth Three does have some advantages."

"Most of them, I fear," said Virginia.

"Yeah, but there's something wrong there."

Virginia asked, "What can be wrong with that kind of technical advance?"

"It isn't only their technical perfection that is wrong. That is fine, and something that Earth One will achieve in the due course of time. There's something else—something basic. Maybe," he grinned, "it is feminine intuition, but it has to be there."

Bronson nodded firmly and then turned to his amplifiers. The closer one he turned upside down on the table and looked into for a time. Then, absently, Bronson reached for a screwdriver and probed into the chassis with the business end.

Virginia gave a cry, "No!"

"No!" cried Virginia, as Bronson probed into the apparatus.

"No?" he echoed, turning slightly to face her. "It's turned off."

Virginia paused. A moment of wait and her worry about Bronson would have been over. After touching the charged electrode in the way he was about to do, Virginia would have been alone and free to go to Earth Three complete with the laboratory, or to wait and see whether One or Three was successful in the imminent warfare and go to whichever emerged victorious.

She knew that Bronson was quite capable of isolating both of them after collecting the only mass of space-resonant elements on Earth One. He would do that as a last resort to save the rest of his world, regardless of whether he received any acclaim or not. And death would be his reward. For once Earth One was safe, Two and Three would perish and both of them with it.

Yet Virginia found admiration in her heart for this man. Bronson, against great odds, had succeeded in coming this far. He may have made an error in his belief that there was something fundamentally wrong with Earth Three but, none the less, he was possessed of a certain drive and purpose that made her admire him.

"All right, Ed," she told him. "I know more about those amplifiers than I could possibly know had I been truly of Earth One."

He turned and faced her slowly.

"I am Virginia—Carlson," she said.

"Carlson?"

"Carlson. I am the woman you contacted with your hybrid space resonator." Then came the rest of the story from beginning to end. "Curse me if you feel like it, Ed Bronson, but what normal human being would care to spend the rest of her life on a dying world—or to open the door of a fine world to the hapless, horrible mutants who have no future beyond their own life-endings?"

Bronson nodded. "I am no judge," he said solemnly. "Offhand it seems wrong to abandon one's friends for one's own safety. But if one cannot really save one's friends from their horrible fate it seems foolish to remain and die through mere loyalty. It's like that old saw about a live coward being better than a dead hero."

"Then you don't condemn me for seeking safety?"

"Who am I to judge?" he said.

"But supposing Earth Three should be successful?"

"That would prove that Earth Three was best fit to survive. Not for one moment, however, do I believe that some higher agency performed this separation-trick to establish the most successful way of running a world.

"Nature—by which I mean natural phenomena—offers survival's choice to many forms of life and living in many ways, and this split in the time stream is but one of them. I swear that we shall know why it happened some day.

"But, Virginia, I am not to arbitrate your life. I am inclined to think that I might have done the same thing. In fact," he said humorously, "I can find nothing really to be angry about. Even your little job of shipping me to Earth Three resulted in our stealing this laboratory."

"But I sent you to Earth Two."

He shook his head. "I arrived from my bedroom on Earth Three—the same room but a nursery in Three's time trail."

"I saw the same room from half-transfer," she said, "and there was that pillar of atomic fire in the sky."

Bronson blinked.

"So," he said with an explosive exhale of breath. "So the fission-train in the earth will work on Earth Three as well as Two."

"What do you mean?" asked the girl.

"Kingston undoubtedly intends to transfer bits of the earth-fire from Two to One and thus destroy both of them. That was a test. They brought it, noted its performance on Three and then carefully shipped the thing back again."

Virginia snorted angrily. "I'd like to ship the entire Alamogordo Fire to Earth Three and let Kingston and Maddox roast!"

Bronson nodded. "But the thing that strikes me the hardest is that only for that very instant of blast was there the chance for time-fission. Then all three worlds have the same phenomena and the same effects. One might think that Three would remain a place where no fission-explosion could take place while on Two all atomic releases of power start the endless fission in the earth."

"But does that help us any?"

"I don't know yet. But you'll help—now?"

"That I will—and willingly."

"Then tell me," said Bronson amusedly, "just what was I about to do?"

"You were about to touch a high-energy electrode that remains hot for hours after the gear is turned off. One of the energizing circuits. It charges itself with space-resonant energy that does not leak off—sort of like a high-capacity condenser of excellent power factor. You can charge it to lethal dose and it may remain so for hours unless it is discharged."

"Why don't they discharge these, then?"

"It takes too long for them to load when they fire 'em up," explained Virginia. "Usually they remain at high charge between 'off' periods."

Ed Bronson looked into the amplifier with a wry glance. "A little knowledge is a dangerous thing," he grunted. He squinted at the electrode, lifted an eyebrow and smiled cynically, "Y' know, there ought to be some easy way of telling when a thing is dangerous.

"Once upon a time that which was dangerous came clearly labeled, like fire, or sabretooth tigers. Later they had to pass laws to get folks to put gasoline in red-coated cans. Nowadays practically anything you open up is dangerous and unless you know what you're doing—"

Virginia smiled. She knew that he was just talking, rambling as he scanned the circuit, wondering what to do next. Then she touched his arm gently.

"Look, Ed," she said. "Let me take this job over. I know my way around these things, even though they are of Earth Three instead of mine. You've got other things to do, doubtless?"

Bronson looked at Virginia quizzically.

"Trust me?" she asked.

He smiled. "I think so," he said.

"You can," she said.

Bronson's smile faded. "Look, kiddo," he said, "there's one thing about being just a little bit selfish that most of the books never get around to mentioning. I'd prefer to have someone working beside me who is a bit selfish and inclined to think of himself first.

"The guy who has—in capitals—a Mission In Life is all too inclined to toss common sense into the ashcan so that his flanged-up ideals are realized. At least you can predict the future course of any character who is logical enough to think of himself.

"So—you've made your gesture and until someone convinces me that a bit of selfishness is absolutely wrong—g'wan!" He grinned. "Go to work so that I can stop sounding like a philosopher."

Virginia looked at him soberly for some moments.

"You don't question the fact that I will grab for the winner?"

"We all hope to play a winner, ginger-girl," he said.

"Yes, but—"

"Virginia, you hope to play a winner. Do you greatly care who really wins so long as all is serene, happy, and peaceful?"

"Only one more requisite," she said wistfully, "I'd like to have it remain that way."

Bronson laughed. "It has been adequately pointed out often enough that the gents who formulated the Declaration of Independence guaranteed only the right to 'pursue' happiness. It is a hopeless quest to seek complete peace and quiet."

"Don't talk like that," she said. "I only meant that I'm not too convinced that your idea about Earth Three having something definitely wrong with it—"

Ed Bronson reached forward and put one hand on each of her shoulders. "Look, youngster," he said with a smile, "I'm no hero. I'm not imbued with the spirit of altruism and self-righteous self-sacrifice."

Virginia looked into his eyes solemnly. "You would have little hesitation before you isolated yourself here on Earth One if—"

"Only because I am dead certain that there is something basically wrong with Earth Three."

Virginia smiled. "As a not-too-innocent bystander," she said seriously, "I'm little sold either way. Earth Two is doomed. That I know because I saw Earth One. But having been trained to the idea of scientific research, I'm inclined to think that Earth Three with its freedom is the right answer.

"Who knows," she continued bitterly, "how many times we might have been close to something that might have led the way to life but were stopped because of an arbitrary decision by someone who felt—by some personal logic—that the phase of science held no answer."

"There is one idea," he said half humorously, "that anything taken without a bit of moderation is not too good. Oh, there are exceptions. One can always find something that must not be taken in moderation—honesty or faith, for instance—in order for the best to evolve. But any pendulum swings from extreme to extreme. And you have been living in an order of one extreme. You naturally think the other extreme is better."

"You wouldn't be generalizing when you claim that Earth Three is wrong somewhere? That you think that Earth Three is too extreme?"

"Extremity, per se, may not be bad," he said. "It is what takes place under extremity that might be dangerous. No, Ginger, I'm baffled right now but you can be certain that, before we get to the end of all this, we'll know the answer."

Virginia smiled. "We seem to have come a long way from the original argument."

"Oh yes." He grinned back at her. "We're both in a mell of a hess right now. It would be a fine thing if we couldn't trust one another. All you seem to want is a secure future and all I want is the same. That we seem to think that this secure future lies in opposite directions is the same factor that makes horse racing interesting. And, like horse racing, we'll find out soon enough who is right."

"I hope it isn't the hard way."

"Virginia, you are willing to take a job on this stuff. You're therefore willing to help the side you think cannot win?"

"If anything is done to aid either side," she said, "and it comes out properly, isn't that a sign that the winning side has every right to succeed?"

"Defining 'A' in terms of 'A'?"

"No. I'm just willing to help get myself away from the certain doom of Earth One."

"In other words," said Ed Bronson, "you'd work as hard for Leader Kingston as you would for me?"

She looked at him squarely. "Ed," she said, "I wouldn't care to trust Leader Kingston." Then she turned from him, shrugged her shoulder out from beneath his hands and faced the upturned amplifier. Beneath the wreath of her hair he noted the blush that tinted the back of her neck.

Bronson took a half step forward. His hands half reached for her shoulders again. Then he paused.

"I'm going to check the mass spectrograph," he said and turned on his heel and left the room.

This, he knew, was no time to question her motives.

As he headed for the laboratory below, this thought crystallized. Questioning her motives would force quick judgment. He knew—and he wondered how he arrived at that sage opinion—that Virginia herself was not aware of the motives that made her keep him from a certain death and now caused her to help him.

Chapter XIV
Explosive!

Now it was silent in the computation laboratory, save for the occasional clicking of the super calculator that lined one wall of the room. Pages and pages of equations were piled high in the file box and Bronson sat in the control console of the big machine and worked. Hour after hour he alternated moments of quick activity over the keyboard with periods of quiet contemplation and reasoning as the answers to his mathematical problems came clicking back.

Dimly he heard the door open behind him and he accepted it vaguely—disinterestedly—because the problem at hand was far more important. He felt her presence beside him and she was silent as she read his notes.

He set up another problem on the keyboard and leaned back, looking up at her.

"Found something?" she asked.

"No," he replied. "Except that the space-resonant elements do not make sense in the mass spectrograph."

"I know," she said. "We've known that for years."

Bronson waved a book. "And I'm a little shocked at the lack of true basic research to be found on Earth Three."

"What?" asked Virginia.

"It seems as though they know a lot," he explained. "But they know no more about this stuff than the nineteen hundreds knew about the electricity they used."

"That's natural," she said. "People are always willing to use something beneficial though they know little about its basic fundamentals. One out of a thousand automobile drivers really knows anything about the internal combustion engine. The rest are merely drivers, controlling a mammoth they know nothing about."

"Well, perhaps," he said. "Also it is entirely possible that what I'm seeking has no true answer."

"You hope to learn why the space-resonant elements cannot be separated?"

"Right," said Bronson. He was silent for some time while he digested the answer that had come clicking from the calculator. Then he sent forth another equation and the machine went to work again. "I'd like to try analysis."

"Won't work. As far as we can tell there is really only one element."

"By analysis," he nodded. He had been reading what Earth Three knew about it and they, too, said as much. "However, the mass spectrograph separates elements according to their atomic masses and according to their atomic charge.

"Now why do we have a dispersion of atomic mass—making the space-resonant series of elements seem to be merely isotopes of the same element—and at the same time get a dispersion of atomic charge, which would make them seem like isobars of different elements?"

"Heaven knows what we can expect in the transuranic series," observed Virginia.

He grunted. "Run down the physical properties of the stable elements," he said, "and you'll run into about every conceivable idea. Metals that melt at room temperature, metals that resist acid and alkali.

"Metals that conduct electricity in proportion to the light falling on them, elements that combine with almost any other element—and elements so valently self-satisfied that they will not even combine with themselves. Elements as hard as all get-out and others that can be cut into stove lengths with a soft thumbnail.

"But," he continued reflectively, "I'm of the opinion that the answer lies here—that this indivisible property of the space-resonant elements is the answer to a lot of questions."

Then Bronson put his head in his hands. "And I'm supposed to find out all this to save my world—when the best brains of that same world in another time-plane have known about the stuff for thirty years and still cannot—"

"That is not fair," she said. "After all, how many years did Enrico Fermi seek the answer for his experiments with the fission of uranium? They numbered a good many transuranic elements before they discovered that these new elements were actually the fissioned products and were well-known elements halfway down the atomic chart."

"That's true," he nodded. "Also it is against all theory that an element should display more than one atomic identity."

"Right. Unless they are incomplete atoms—a house built of brickbats."

Bronson shrugged. "I'm trying that."

"How?" puzzled Virginia.

"I've got the mass spectrograph running again but each slit is loaded to the scuppers with neutron absorber."

"What do you expect?" asked Virginia.

"I don't really know. I sort of hope it may lead to something. Come on—let's try it."

Taking his last three pages of calculations, Ed Bronson led the way to the analytic laboratory....

Leader Kingston smiled grimly at Maddox and shoved the button home. "That'll fix 'em!" he said savagely.

On Earth Two the pillar of fire flickered a measurable bit—and the downtown district of New York City vomited flame in a thunderous roar. To the stratosphere billowed the ice cap, followed instantly by an up-reaching column of incandescent gas.

Into the vitals of the rock the gnawing atomic flame went and perceptibly—perceptibly to some all-powerful deity that could withstand a holocaust which put the sun to shame—the crater expanded as the substance of Earth Two fed the atomic flame.

Kingston set the steering control once more and shoved the button. The Mall between the Washington Monument and the Capitol erupted in another atomic cancer to feed on Earth Two. The buildings that lined the Mall were blasted to bits—the National Archives, the Smithsonian Institution, all of them gone in one mighty blast.

Then, as the fury of blast subsided, the pillar of fire undulated to the sky. It fed, then, on the inert substance of a dead city for, as in Manhattan, no man remained alive to see.

With cruel disregard for humanity, Leader Kingston set the dials once more and the acres of land enclosed by Chicago's Loop roared skyward. The edges of the crater rimmed Lake Michigan and the waters of the lake began to pour toward the breach. They did not reach the ravening crater for they turned into steam long before they could fall across the lip of the crater.

From Lake Bluff to Gary the lake-front was a scene of molten death.

"That's but the beginning," said Kingston. "Four will become eight and eight will become sixteen. It will not be long before they are reaching one another."

"You'll have a lot of the space-resonant crystals to pass along to Earth One, though," said Maddox.

"We will apply the same principle," said Kingston. "One brings two and each brings two more. My men on Earth One will assemble the four subcritical masses tomorrow for instructions," said Kingston. "This is the one weak link. But once we start, we can move the stuff like fury."

"What do you fear?" asked Maddox.

"Bronson! He has your laboratory. Complete. He is well hidden somewhere and, until we can locate him, we are treading on dangerous ground. For I know that he is keeping an eye on everything we do. And until we locate him we can do nothing."

"Why doesn't he do something, then?"

Kingston laughed bitterly. "Probably because he doesn't quite know what to do."

Maddox grinned. "Also because you've got the key to Earth One. And," he said grimly, "it might be that he has been ignorant until just now when you've shown him how to fight this war."

Kingston whitened in fear. He shook his fist at the flaming horror on the viewer plate and said, "I wish Bronson were in that!"

Virginia Carlson reeled back from the viewer with a cry. Bronson left his work and came to stand beside her.

"What?" he asked.

Slowly Virginia shook her head. "Kingston has just transmitted a bit of the atomic flame to New York," she said.

Bronson made the natural error. To him, New York was New York and he considered no other city. What stopped him was the belief that Kingston could not transmit anything across the barrier without the presence of a focal mass.

"How?" he asked Virginia.

"With the space resonator," she said.

"But there is no focal mass."

"In New York?" replied Virginia in surprise. "There must be several thousand."

"But—oh! It was the New York of Earth Two."

"Yes."

Bronson looked out of the window and shook his head. "I find it difficult to believe that this terrain is not my own world," he said. "And yet it is, in a sense."

Then he turned from the window to face Virginia. "Ginger-girl," he said slowly, "I know what is wrong with Earth Three!"

Virginia swung the steering control swiftly until a distant view of New York was visible. "That is what is wrong with Earth Three," she said bitterly. "Avaricious, hateful and cruel."

Bronson shook his head. "You're not fair," he said. "He's done nothing that you or I would not do to protect our own worlds. And," smiled Bronson, "remember that Earth Two is already doomed."

Virginia whirled on him. "Because a man is slated to die as all men are, is that an excuse to commit murder?"

"No," he said. "But life is still a matter of the survival of the fittest. I deplore Kingston's act but remember that Kingston knows that it is either kill or be killed."

"Then there is nothing wrong with Earth Three," snapped Virginia with deep bitterness.

"Oh but there is. Virginia, on your world, where every scientific endeavour is directed along the one line of safety in the face of that pillar of fire at Alamogordo, does your government know the location of all equipment?"

"Of course," she said. "Save for a very minute percentage of stuff that has been lost, strayed or stolen."

He turned to the screen. "Did anybody ever think of that?" he asked, pointing to the fire that was consuming Manhattan.

"Yes—but where would we put it?" she asked.

"On the moon," he said simply.

"But there is no focal mass of space resonant elements on the moon," she objected.

"There could have been," he said, "if Earth Two had proceeded to develop the rocket! But no, since no planet is habitable."

"That isn't all," said Virginia. "Earth Three has developed the transmission resonator to the highest degree. We've never been able to speed it up. They can transmit anything in a matter of microseconds. Ours takes hours sometimes.

"Remember, if we start to shove that pillar of raw energy through a resonator of our type we must build it to withstand raw atomic energy for a long period. But tell me what is wrong with Earth Three."

He frowned. "Remember the day I nearly killed myself because I was poking into an amplifier without knowing all about it?"

"Yes."

"In similar sense, Earth Three is plunging forward into a sea of uncharted danger. Rapid progress in the face of high competition. No control whatsoever. In the cast of Earth Two, progress has been hampered because it has had too much control.

"Had you been free to tinker and investigate the transmission bands you'd have discovered Earth Three and you might have had the idea of rotating that Alamogordo Flame into Earth Three.

"As of now, Virginia, tell me—could Earth Two reduce all of its space-resonant elements to subcritical masses in a case of danger?"

"We could, save for those that were lost, as I've said before."

Bronson smiled cryptically. "Can Leader Kingston?"

Virginia shook her head. She recalled the myriad uses that Earth Three had developed for the space resonant elements. Each home with many devices, each device containing a supercritical mass.

To eliminate entirely all critical masses of the dangerous elements would be the exact equal to a complete breakdown of all means of transportation and communication. For the space resonator had replaced in nearly all but isolated cases the common automobile, telephone, train, radio and allied arts.

Such a project was impossible to contemplate, and even less possible to accomplish in any reasonable time. It would require the rebuilding of the former modes of life—almost a return to horse-and-buggy days.

"But every science has its danger," objected Virginia.

Bronson nodded. "But remember that every science grows like a tree. One does not start on a high technical plane."

"But what has that to do with it?"

"Just this," explained Bronson patiently, "In earlier days no man could develop anything too dangerous to his fellows if it got out of hand. Many embryonic chemists have left the face of the earth in a gout of smoke and flame but, when they left, they took only a small section of the neighborhood with them.

"Here, then, we have Alamogordo and the Bomb. It took the combined resources of a nation, its people and years of study and work to develop the atomic bomb. Obviously this is no backyard project like the nitration of glycerine.

"But here we have Earth Three," he continued, "plunging forward without control—a juggernaut with no one at the helm. In their homes, in their laboratories, in their very lives, they have supercritical masses of the space-resonant elements. Leader Kingston has just shown us how he hopes to destroy both Earth One and Two to leave Three supreme."

"In doing that he has given us the answer we seek. For in his attack," said Bronson exultantly, "he has displayed not only his weakness but the fundamental weakness of a culture based upon complete freedom. Not that freedom is wrong. Freedom is an ideal, and complete freedom will be attained only when every man can assume the responsibility of being noble."

"I'm not quite certain," said Virginia.

Bronson laughed. "How long would it be before one of Kingston's men discover the secret of unlocking the energy of the atom with a gadget the size of your wrist watch? Hah! Every man his own atom-bomb!" he snorted. "Well, remember this, Virginia, on Earth Three every chunk of space-resonant material is more deadly than the Alamogordo Flame!"

Chapter XV
Moment of Crisis

Grinning wolfishly, Bronson spoke.

"The next problem," he said, "is the job of getting back to Earth One."

"How can we?"

"Who has the key?" Bronson asked.

"Kingston."

"Then we proceed to grab Leader Kingston and apply bamboo splinters under the fingernails or place a rat on his bare tummy, placing a bowl on top of the rat, and then building a small fire on top of the bowl. In other words, we shall—ah—urge is the word—urge him to reveal his method of getting in touch with his bunch on Earth One."

Virginia shuddered.

Bronson turned to the steering controls and located Kingston. Then, standing near the focal volume, Bronson motioned for the girl to throw the switch. Kingston appeared instantly and, before the Leader could get his wits together, Ed Bronson swung a heavy fist with all the power of his big body behind it. Kingston went down like a log.

He awakened to the drenching of cold water from a bucket. He strained against adhesive tape and glared.

"Take it easy, Kingston," said Bronson. "I've got the controls set to drop you into the Alamogordo Flame if you get nasty."

Kingston paled.

"What I want from you is the key to Earth One!"

"That you'll never get!"

"Yes I will."

"No you won't."

Bronson snorted. "Want to make a little bet? You can save yourself a lot of grief if you give in right now. Or would you rather be screaming for mercy later?"

"What can you do?" sneered Kingston.

Bronson chuckled. "The Chinese are accused of developing a number of fancy tortures," he said. "I've also known a fiction writer who used an incident to show the strength of his character's will power.

"This fellow, who used to tinker with radio on the side, decided that any man who could grab a couple of hundred volts and not quiver a muscle because a sudden motion would be as deadly, would be displaying a nervous control seldom realized. Now I'd guess his idea to have been impossible. But it gives me to think.

"Do you suppose you could stand a mild electrocution? Say a hundred volts at twenty cycles? Not enough to kill, for we'll insert a current-limiting resistance to prevent electrocution, but enough to make life most uncomfortable. The torture of the condemned will have nothing on what you will suffer, Kingston."

Kingston smiled wearily. "It will do you no good," he said. "The thing is set up like the time lock on a safety vault. No one can breach it."

"Big talk," snorted Bronson. He turned from the bound man and rummaged in a bench drawer for wire and parts. A variable-voltage transformer, some alternating current meters and a few lengths of wire were strewn over the table top. Bronson began to connect them into a circuit.

"We'll find out how your resistance is," he told Kingston over his shoulder.

Kingston laughed nastily, Virginia screamed. Bronson whirled—and Kingston was gone!

Bronson leaped to the viewer controls and spun the dial to Kingston's official quarters. The viewer showed a technician just in the act of spinning the steering dials in a random whirl like a man locking a combination safe.

Kingston fell a-sprawl, still bound, against Maddox, who had come with him. Maddox removed the bonds and Kingston fingered the amulet on his wrist with pride. "That was quick," he said.

"Had to be," said Maddox. "I knew that the instant you disappeared from Bronson's laboratory he'd leap to the viewer to see your laboratory.

So once you arrived, we both came here and Tony spun the dials so that Bronson can't follow us by reading the calibration."

"That isn't all," chuckled Kingston. "Now we know how to reach Bronson!"

Bronson turned from the controls unhappily. "How did he do that?" he asked plaintively.

Virginia shook her head. "Wrong culture or no," she said, "Earth Three seems to take all the tricks."

Bronson nodded wearily. He put head in hands and worried visibly — and was taken out of it when a bell tinkled on the wall. Bronson leaped to his feet with a shout.

"Maybe we're not licked yet," he said. "That was the automatic mass spectro-analyzer."

He left the room and returned quickly with a sheaf of papers.

"They call 'em space-resonant," he said with a wry chuckle, "but I call 'em symbiotic."

"Meaning?"

"Why, it seems as though we have a closed system of radioactivity here," he said.

"But the space-resonant elements are only faintly radioactive," objected Virginia.

"According to outside detectors," he said. "But this is an internally closed system. There are two basic elements and two isotopes of each, all operating in a closed system."

"How?"

He handed her a sheet of paper containing nuclear equations.

① $121_A^{227} + 0_n^1 \;-\!-\!\!\to\; 121_A^{280}$

② $121_A^{280} - 1_e^0 \;-\!-\!\!\to\; 122_B^{280}$

③ $122_B^{280} - 0_n^1 \;-\!-\!\!\to\; 122_B^{279}$

④ $122_B^{279} + 1_e^0 \;-\!-\!\!\to\; 121_A^{279}$

"Call 'em 'A' and 'B', with respective atomic number of one hundred and twenty-one and one hundred and twenty-two and respective atomic weights of two hundred and seventy-nine and two hundred and eighty," he explained. "Then Element A absorbs a neutron, becoming heavy Element A since its atomic weight is increased by one.

"The heavy Element A then emits a negative electron which raises the nuclear charge by one and the element becomes Element B. Element B then emits a neutron which makes it light Element B.

"Light Element B captures an electron lowering the nuclear charge and retransmuting the element back to normal Element A. The neutrons and electrons are passed back and forth within the mass and seldom escape, therefore the space-resonant elements are believed to be only mildly radioactive."

"Yes?"

Miles away and across the barrier in time Kingston and Maddox listened avidly.

"So we can guess what happened at Alamogordo," said Bronson exultantly.

"I don't see it," she said.

"Well, Element A is so avid an absorber of neutrons that a microscopic impurity will destroy the K-factor of a supercritical mass of plutonium or uranium," he said. "That would prevent the Alamogordo Bomb from exploding."

"Element B, on the other hand, emits a torrent of neutrons, enough to raise the K-factor to a terribly high degree, which caused such violence that the bomb was hot enough to start fission in the earth. A balance of the elements A and B cancels out and therefore we have the normal explosion experienced in Earth One."

"But how did it happen?"

"When the subcritical masses of uranium came together on Alamogordo Day, the fission started throughout the mass. Also present—we know now—is the capture of neutrons by unfissioned atoms which raise the element's mass, and the other fission products hitting this element raise its charge. Space-resonant elements resulted in those sub-microseconds of initial fission.

"So, in one section of the mass, an abundance of Element A was produced, which stopped the explosion. In another section, Element B was produced, which increased its violence. Now the energies produced within the fissioning bomb are high enough to cause a warp in the space-time continuum. This warp permitted one section to die out while the other increased almost without limit."

"I'm beginning to understand," nodded Virginia. "We then had three different levels of energy."

"And three widely-varied levels of entropy," added Bronson. "So widely varied that they could not exist in the same time-space plane. Thus the fission in time that produced the three time-planes. How widespread these areas of separation extend we may never know.

"All I can assume is that space-time is strained and will return as soon as the energy put into the separation is used up. Sort of like an upthrown stone," he mused. "It goes up until the energy put into throwing it is used up against the force of gravity.

"Then it comes down—and the three time-planes separate until the energy put into the separation was used up and then they begin to fall toward one another."

Kingston turned to Maddox. "That also explains why no one knew of this split for so long. And why it is getting easier and easier to cross the barrier. The three time-planes are approaching one another."

Maddox nodded. "And that means that we must see the other time-planes destroyed. If they come together and find interference—all will die!"

"Right," said Kingston. His hand fingered the button while his other hand turned the steering control. Maddox looked into the viewer. "Hurry!" he exploded. Kingston looked.

Ed Bronson was walking across the laboratory toward the transmission panel, saying "... and that brings one thing to mind, Ginger. If they grabbed Kingston they know where we are!"

He spun the controls quickly and pressed the button. At the same instant Kingston pressed his own button. The viewplate that showed Bronson and Virginia in Maddox's laboratory erupted in a holocaust of flame that blinded Kingston and Maddox.

"Did we?" asked Kingston, rubbing his eyes.

"We can't know," said Maddox. "But look. If we got them we can find out."

"How?"

"Collect your space-resonant elements on Earth One," said Maddox. "Then send another set across and use one of them to erupt Central City—right where Bronson's home is."

"What good will that do?" asked Kingston.

"We can watch it," explained Maddox. "And if it is returned to Earth Two, we'll know that Bronson is alive somewhere and watching."

Kingston nodded with a smile of appreciation.

The laboratory building was askew, its windows shattered and its outer surface scarred. It had been close. Perhaps the only thing that saved them was the fact that they were closer to the focal volume of the transmitter in the laboratory than Kingston was.

At any rate the unbelievably microscopic instant of the beginning of the atomic flame intended to destroy them utterly had been all that building caught. For Bronson had sent it skirling into time-space and it was on the way out as the glimmering of deadly flame started to come in.

But that brief touch of incandescent death had charred the woodwork of the outside of the building. It had cracked the glass and it had jarred its very structure.

The inhabitants were in bad shape. Bronson was sprawled on the floor. Virginia was crumpled over a desk. Both were unconscious. And, creeping deeper into their skin, was the ruddy color of bad burn.

Hours later they were dark with burn and still unconscious. They knew nothing.

They did not know that Kingston's men on Earth One were beginning to assemble the masses in Ed Bronson's collection of radioisotopic phosphor.

Then a bell tinkled gently. Bronson stirred and groaned. The bell tinkled once more. Bronson stirred again—painfully. Another tinkle—

Virginia awakened, opened her eyes vaguely and wondered what had happened.

The bell rang insistently. "Ed—Ed Bronson!" she shouted. "The detector!"

"Detector?" he asked dully.

"They're assembling the space-resonant elements on Earth One!"

The bell broke into an insistent clamoring. Ed picked himself from the floor and looked at the gear. The cascaded amplifiers, incapable of detecting the presence of subcritical masses on Earth One, had sufficient gain to trigger the alarm when Earth One's bits of space resonant elements were collected into critical mass.

Bronson spun the dials of the viewer.

There before him was the familiar laboratory of his own home and four men standing before his bench, upon which stood the crystalline mass.

"Now!" breathed Ed Bronson.

Chapter XVI
A World at Stake

Uncertainly Virginia paused. "Ed," she said.

"Huh?" he asked, turning.

"You're going to—"

"I must."

She smiled and took a deep breath. Bronson looked at her quizzically. It was obvious that something had happened that had pleased her—or convinced her of something, but what it might be eluded him.

"Look, Ginger, we haven't much time. I've got to get going—and you know what to do."

She nodded, her eyes bright and intent upon him. "Ed," she said in a quiet voice, "I've been both selfish and opportunist, wanting security at any price. But you are willing to trust me with the future of Earth One. That, too, proves the worth of—worth of—of—"

"Forget it," he said softly. "If we win it will prove the right of Earth One to survive."

Then he turned to the machine again. "I've got to go!"

She came up behind him, turned him around and kissed him. "Go," she said. "And as you go, Ed, remember that I've made up my mind. I'm going with you—all the way!"

He smiled down at her. "I know," he said cryptically. Then he turned and snapped the button.

He landed in his own laboratory amid the four minions of Kingston. The suddenness of his appearance sent them flying in four directions. He whirled and reached for the assembled blocks of the space-resonant elements on the bench, to separate them again.

He was hit from behind by one of the thugs and staggered against the bench. Then the other three were upon him.

Only Bronson's sheer size and physical power saved him from instant annihilation. He fought them off, hitting them hard but taking a murderous amount of punishment. He kicked one away, traded blows with the second, turned to drive a hard fist into the face of the third—and nearly fell forward on his face as the blow passed through nothing!

Bronson tried desperately to fight off the thugs.

In the big laboratory on Earth Two Virginia coldly and viciously clubbed Kingston's hired hand over the back of the head with a heavy end-wrench as the fellow was still staggering forward from the effort against Bronson.

Bronson blinked and recovered from his stagger. He lashed out at the nearest, just as Virginia grabbed another to give him the same treatment. One of the two remaining jerked a gun from his pocket and fired wildly. Bronson ducked under the gun hand and shouldered the thug cruelly in the pit of the stomach.

The gun dropped to the floor and there was a three-way dive for it. Bronson cracked his head against the nearer man's jaw, drove a fist into the other's face, and grabbed the wrist of the first one again. A gun appeared in the second man's hand.

Bronson jerked the wrist and the man staggered forward in front of Bronson just as the other thug fired. Ed felt the man's body twitch and he coldly lifted a foot, set it in the small of the stricken man's back and hurled him forward against the gun wielder. Behind him went Bronson but the gun wielder disappeared.

Virginia's quick end-wrench came down hard and then she had three of them lined up on the floor, taped helplessly with adhesive tape.

She scribbled a quick note and sent it through—and an instant later Bronson had the mass of crystals separated into their four parts.

He breathed deeply as he read the note. It did present a problem. He had one corpse on his hands and three other undesirables collected in the laboratory on Earth Two. Also, here he was safe on Earth One again with the crystals separated. He held the key to security!

But there was Earth Three, still whole and alive. How simple it would have been to ignore Three—Bronson admitted that Virginia might have had to suffer the fortunes of war if the fate of an entire world rested upon the decision.

But Bronson knew that, unless two of the three worlds were exterminated, all would die in a cosmic explosion when they began to reappear on the same time-plane.

Furthermore, he knew that Kingston was quite prepared to maintain a viewer on each of Ed Bronson's sections of crystal until they were reassembled again. For the very key that opened the portal was as deadly as the Alamogordo Flame....

A hard knock came at the door. Ed turned, puzzled, and went through his house to open it.

Captain Norris of the police strode into the room with a sour expression.

"What are you running here?" he demanded. "Where are the four birds that came in here a few minutes ago. Where have you been?"

Norris strode through the house until he came to the laboratory. He looked down at the body of Kingston's henchman and his eyebrows beetled. "This smacks of murder," he said flatly.

"It—"

"Self-defense," said Norris sourly. "Tell it to the judge." He looked around. "Where are the other three?"

"See here, Norris," snapped Bronson. "When I came to you about the invaders of earth you slapped me in the booby hatch. What would you say if I gave you proof?"

"It will have to be mighty good," snapped Norris.

From separate pockets Ed Bronson took the four bits of crystal. He set them side by side on the bench.

"Virginia," he said, knowing that she was listening. "Now!"

And his hands scooped the crystals together.

"Who are you—hey!" exploded Norris. They had come across the barrier and were standing in the laboratory building. In the viewer stood Virginia Carlson. She smiled through at them and showed them that she had once more separated the bits of crystal.

"What goes on?" Norris stormed.

"You are now on Earth Two," said Bronson. "And if you want to get back play it smart."

"Don't threaten me—who are these?"

"Three thugs from Earth Three."

"Oh fine," jeered Norris. "This sounds like a real game. Now look—"

"You look," snapped Bronson. He set the controls and snapped the button and the scene outside of the laboratory disappeared. In its place was a tall pillar of flame.

"That," said Bronson, "is the pillar of atomic flame at Alamogordo, caused on Earth Two by the original Manhattan Project experiment in Nineteen forty-five." He spun the dials once more, and the city of Washington was visible at a distance. Its pillar of flame roared high into the sky. "That's Earth Two, Washington," he snapped at Norris.

"But what can you do?" asked Norris, completely dumbfounded.

"I can fight back—now," said Bronson harshly. "And you can sit in a corner and figure out a means for a man to come to official quarters to tell of an extra-space invasion without being clapped in the nuthouse!"

He turned from Norris and adjusted the steering controls.

His hand came down on the button.

And Earth Three Washington erupted in a massive incandescent flame.

Kingston shouted in anger as the report came. He twirled his own dials, found a response and pressed the button.

He cried, "*Orders!* Everyone possessing a Type One transmitter, help spread the atomic fire on Earth Two!"

Out across the face of Earth Three went the orders and the mobilized hundreds of thousands of people started their space resonators.

It was furious work. Bronson whirled the dials until the plane of view looked down upon Earth Two from several thousand miles above. From this point, Bronson knew that Kingston—from whatever hideout he was in—was directing a full-scale attack against Earth Two. The lights twinkled like a field of fireflies.

Bronson knew that his own attempts were pitiful against Kingston's massed attack.

Maybe Virginia was right. Maybe, in the final analysis Earth Three did hold all the tricks and would win. But whether or not he won or lost Bronson was going to fight to the bitter end. He directed his fire against Earth Three—and saw two disappear as one flared forth.

Bitterly, Bronson nodded. Kingston was well staffed. He could without difficulty set a number of his stations to the job of sending back upon Earth Two the few fires that Bronson could start. He was one man fighting a world well-armed—a gnat batting its head against a wall of polished chromium steel.

Bronson stopped punching the button with a gesture of sheer futility.

And from the vantage point above Earth Two, his viewer showed a spreading holocaust that threatened to cover the entire globe from pole to pole. It would be but a matter of time before a gout of flame and horror erased him and removed all resistance to Kingston's plans. Switching the scene to Earth Three, Bronson saw that the pitifully few dots of flame had been removed.

Which was right? A world playing with death in myriad or a world so conservative that it had not advanced to the point where it could turn the tables?

Bronson shook his head hopelessly.

The incandescent, flaming curtain almost obscured Earth Two now. The sky was alight and the rumblings and roarings shook the rocks. Torrents of wind howled back and forth and carried minute bits of the flame with them, feeding on the very air that carried them. They landed and they started their own fires in a million smaller craters.

Bronson shook his head. There was not much point in making even one last gesture. He hit the control panel with his fist and slumped in his chair. He took one last look at Earth Two and felt futility once more at the spreading of the atomic horror.

And then Bronson sat bolt upright. A last gesture! Before he had rushed in where angels fear to tread!

He looked at the equipment and shook his head. But equipment made well can withstand a terrific overload for a brief time. Even the most delicate of component parts require measurable time between application of a tremendous overload and ultimate failure.

His left hand spun the dials and his right hand tuned the transmitter.

He hoped for a break—and he knew also that this was IT in capital letters. If it worked he was the dead winner. If it failed he was doomed to remain on Earth Two to watch the arrival of atomic death.

But he had no other choice. Facing death either way he'd best go out making a try.

Kingston grunted sourly at the visi-plate and pointed out a faint arc at one edge. "What's that?" he asked. "Do we need a new tube at this crucial moment?"

"No."

"Then what is it?"

Maddox turned the dials a bit and the arc came out of the frame clearly enough to display a disc. Faint, unreadable, but none the less a definite pattern.

Maddox looked at it carefully and then retreated the plane of view to many thousands of miles into deep space. Right out to the limit of his range he went.

And there were three discs, all of a size. One was, of course, the flaming Earth Two.

"We're approaching!" yelled Kingston. "Those other discs are Earth One and Three."

"But—"

"When their energy levels approach one another it will be unnecessary to employ a depth of penetration correction!" snapped Kingston. "For they'll all be on the same level."

"And when they do—we'll all go skyward."

The communicator clicked and Kingston read the tape. Then with a nasty chuckle, Kingston spun the dials and looked in upon Ed Bronson. "Darn few live pieces of element left on Two," sneered Kingston. "Made picking him out so much easier!"

"Yes," said Maddox dubiously, "but what in the devil is he doing?"

"He's—heavens!" screamed Kingston. His hand stabbed for the button like a striking snake.

And down upon Ed Bronson's stolen laboratory there descended a torrent of raw energy. In through the space resonator it came and it should have boiled out in the terrible holocaust that produced sunlike pillars of roaring atomic destruction.

Instead, the sheer energy came roaring in through the supercritical mass of space-resonant elements in Ed Bronson's stolen laboratory and entered the transmitter circuits, which were wide open to accept—nay, draw—all available energy from whatever source was available.

Into the circuits went the torrent of energy. It drove the focal volume out and out and out even beyond Ed Bronson's faintest hope. It expanded the volume and then energized the transmission circuits.

And Earth Two—atomic holocaust and all—disappeared from the time-plane it had occupied for so many years. There was a shrinking—but no one was there to record this collapse of the special plane—and at once, a joining, and though it seemed as though Earth One had come into full visibility, this impression was due to the time-fields joining with the original plane.

Virginia Carlson, alone and wondering on Earth One, alternately watched her wrist watch and smoked furiously.

She watched the second hand creep to its appointed meeting with the top of the dial, and she scooped the space-resonant elements into the palms of her hands. This must be done quickly, so very swiftly lest Kingston manage to get through with more than could be handled safely.

Zero!

Virginia clapped her hands together, creating an instantaneous supercritical mass.

**Virginia clapped her hands together
and there was a flash of flame.**

Intolerable heat burned her hands. There was a flash of flame that blinded her and there was the rush and clatter of debris showering the laboratory, shattering windows, and pelting her mercilessly. A heavy something crashed against her skull and drove her to the floor.

Her eyes opened and the space-resonant crystals, crushed by the impact, sifted through her inert fingers and mingled with the powdery untouchably-hot debris that was inch-deep on the floor....

Leader Kingston's hand was stopped in mid-strike. He and his laboratory flamed into instant incandescence as matter was rent to mix with the raving splitting atoms of intolerable explosion.

For close were the temporal paths and the catastrophic energy of Earth Two found its outlet through the myriad of open paths furnished by the millions of commercially-used bits of space-resonant elements. From each of the crystals there poured a torrent of overwhelming flame that of itself formed more of the space-resonant elements.

The excess in entropy of Earth Two forced the transfer regardless of true tuning—as a nearby radio station will blast through to audibility regardless of the position of the dial—or, perhaps better, the excess in entropy level sought the deficient level of entropy as a north magnetic pole seeks the south magnetic pole. Water—or energy—finds its own stable level.

So from the machines that employed space resonant elements on Earth Three there poured the flaming substance and the excess of energy, to spread in one mighty explosion that rent space itself, but died when there was no more substance left to convert.

And with the release of the temporal strains, there came once more that imperceptible withdrawal of strife in the cosmic planes. Now all was at stable rest and there remained but one time-plane. That plane contained Earth One and all that belonged to it.

It contained a man hurled back through the space-resonant transmission equipment from Earth Two, from the one place where the atomic destruction had yet to reach, to the one and only place upon Earth One where space-resonant elements existed. And they alone had been tuned to Ed Bronson's stolen equipment, and held in supercritical mass for that bare instant of transfer by a woman's hands.

Burned, bruised and battered, Ed Bronson and Virginia Carlson would soon awaken from their unconsciousness to look into one another's eyes and wonder.